a novella

by Stephen Meier

ISBN: 1-4392-1633-9
ISBN-13: 9781439216330

Visit www.booksurge.com to order additional copies.

I would like to thank my family and all those who have always believed in me…

"No you cannot touch the merchandise!" Gavin shouted with ill intentions.

"Well, her tits are a little smaller than I had hoped."

"So fucking buy her some new ones! Fuck! Are you kidding me?" said Gavin staring hard and uneasy at a slightly older and overweight man who was eyeing a beautiful Czech girl sitting across the room of a very lavish Hotel Suite.

Gavin was cleary agitated and on edge. This one was very different from the others. None had been this hard, and the phone call the night before hadn't helped matters.

After she hung up, he couldn't get back to sleep.

Worse, he couldn't stop his mind from racing with horrible thoughts and fantasies.

"I don't really know if she's going to do."

"Are you fisting me?! She's fucking nails man, and the best fucking pussy you'll ever get! Look at you! You're fucking disgusting and this girl is willing to be your wife, cook, clean, suck your little dick, whatever you desire! Guys would kill for a girl like this!"

"Whoa there, calm down! What's your deal?" the older man asked obviously surprised by the aggressiveness.

Gavin shook his head in utter frustration.

He couldn't help but think, why didn't he say something last night?

Just something.

Anything.

"I sure would like to touch her," said Dale with that look of a fifty something year old conservative man who obviously stays up late at night looking at porn on the net.

Gavin was astonished.

"Man, this isn't a new car. What the fuck?!" he shouted getting up and heading to the other side of the room, distancing himself from Dale before he did something he would regret. He looked over at Simona, a twenty-two year old knockout, with jet black croppped hair. Very hip and chic, sexier than hell. The kind of girl whom if you spent five minutes with you would be convinced was the devil, but still would want to fuck whether you are a guy or a girl.

She nodded her head in agreement.

"Alright man, but you're pissing me off!"

Dale looked like Christmas came early.

He actually began to loosen up his fingers.

"Man, you are a freak!"

"Hey, settle down. I'm the one who is about to give you a shit load of money. I think the least you could do is let me touch her, see her up close."

Gavin smiled, bit his lower lip and motioned for the girl to come over.

She did, walking over to Dale like a girl on a mission.

All the girls had an amazing ability to make these guys fumble over themselves.

They all wanted a shot at a better life.

Misch was no different.

Standing in front of Dale he immediately began fondling her.

It was sad, disgusting, and pathetic, just as you would picture a man who got no ass to be.

6

Gavin watched for awhile until visions of another girl, Katka, replaced those of this girl.

Katka was a striking beauty with blond razor cut hair worn stylishly messy, hard cheek bones and lines, and a smile that said heaven and hell.

Eyes that said home.

The visions were quick, flashing, like jabs from a boxer.

They stung.

And deep.

To the bone.

Quickly he got up and headed to the bathroom to splash water on his face, hoping to wash away the pain.

Simona watched very closely with great concern.

He's gotten worse she thought to herself.

The last couple hadn't gone so smooth, and with what happened last week, this could prove to be fatal.

Once in the bathroom and standing in front of the mirror, Gavin stared hard at himself and began talking aloud, wondering how he got here.

He no longer recognized the man staring back at him.

He had lost his way.

And the words Simona had said the week after it all began echoed in his head, "Don't ask the questions in which you're not prepared to hear the answers."

He shook his head in complete despair.

"Jesus, what have I done?"

He had been in town about a week when he first saw her. He was getting coffee at a little shop around the corner from his new apartment when he first laid eyes on her.

Absolutely stunning.

One of those girls that you set eyes on and feel like you've found what you've been looking for your entire life.

He actually stopped in his tracks and felt like the wind had been knocked out of him.

Their eyes met, held and then she smiled. A smile that he would think about all day long. A smile that would make him forget about the past couple of months and what had brought him over here. Quite an accomplishment considering what had played out.

But he had always been shy at first and the idea of getting rejected was way too much for him to handle at the moment. Everything was still too fresh.

Even when she turned back in line and caught his stare, almost inviting him to say hello, he just couldn't do it.

God, he wanted to talk to her.

She was truly captivating.

So he made it his point to be back for coffee every morning at the same time, hoping that she would be there.

And every morning she was, and every morning they would make eye contact, live a thousand years in those moments, and he would watch her walk away.

Never saying hello.

Until one day…

Gavin stood there staring at the mirror.

He thought to himself that he really did look like shit. He had bags under his eyes, and his face looked of stress, pain, and hard living. He had been hitting the booze pretty hard, unable to drink away the visions.

Suddenly there was a knock at the door, and without waiting for a response, Simona came in.

Gavin immediately shook his head at her.

"That's the best you could get?" Gavin asked motioning to the girl in the other room, obviously not impressed at all, especially given the high quality of girls that they had been dealing in.

"Gavin, the girls are scared! They're afraid they'll all end up like Meeka."

"Don't say that name!"

They stared at one another. A very cold, icy, stare.

Then Gavin's face turned desolate.

"Please, don't say that name," he pleaded as if he was asking for leniency.

Simona took a deep breath.

"Gavin, you need to chill out."

He didn't say anything.

"Please, this isn't good for business."

He laughed.

He didn't know what else to do.

"Seriously, what has gotten into you? You're totally fucked today?"

He looked at her in almost desperation.

It took him awhile to even say the words.

"I got a call last night."

"And?"

"…it was Katka."

The mere mention of her name seemed to tear him apart and strain him considerably.

Simona's face flushed with excitement, surprise, and ultimately fear.

"What did she say?"

"She didn't. She just cried."

Simona didn't say a word.

Gavin shook his head in disgust and pain.

"So that's my fucking problem! That's the first call i've ever gotten, and all she did was cry."

All he could think about was the whimpering on the other end of the line and how his heart felt like it was tearing into pieces.

He didn't know what to say either, which probably made it worse.

What could he say after all?

His eyes began to tear up.

"I'm going to wrap this shit up," he said. "I don't know what it is with this guy but he's really pushing my buttons today."

Quickly he wiped his face with a towel and walked back into the main room of the suite.

As he did, he noticed that Dale had his hands all over the girl. Again the girl's face flashed back to Katkas.

That's all he could see.

It was tattooed on his soul.

All the drinks in the world couldn't help him.

"Alright man, that's enough! Get your hands off her!"

Dale sat her on his lap.

"I said stop fucking touching her!"

"Calm down, I am."

"So, are we ready to do business or what?"

"I'm not sure. I mean I guess she's pretty good looking, but..."

"Are you saying no? You've never seen pussy this good, nor will you ever again in the rest of your fucking miserable life."

"Relax. Jesus! I'm just wondering if you have anything else?"

Gavin was shocked as all hell to hear this statement.

"You're kidding me right? You're fucking kidding me?"

There was a long pause.

"I thought I would have my choice."

"This isn't fucking Baskin Robbins! You said you wanted the best. She's the best I got."

Dale looked over to Simona.

"What about her?"

Gavin smiled. It was an evil one and he thought how fitting this would be.

Perfect symmetry.

"Sure, take her. Please."

Dale smiled.

"Really?! You don't need her?" he asked.

The question seemed quizzical to Gavin, but he brushed it off.

"No, not at all. I can jerk myself off."

The words seemed to hurt Simona. They were cruel and unexpected. Lacerating.

"Wow...!" Dale said beginning to laugh. "They said with you that everyone was for sale."

"What?"

It was all in the way Gavin said it.

There was malice in his voice.

"What did you just say?" Gavin said approaching Dale in such a way that created a tension so great it was suffocating.

Again nothing.

"Why did you say that?"

"....just heard that you and Katka, kind of had something."

"Really?"

"Yes."

"And who told you that?"

He didn't answer, and it was obvious that he wasn't going to answer.

He just wanted to rattle Gavin.

This bothered Gavin to the core.

"Why would you even fucking bring that up right now?"

Again Dale didn't answer.

"Why!?" Gavin screamed inches away from his face.

Things were tense.

Simona jumped in.

"I'm not an option."

Gavin backed off, his eyes ablaze, never leaving Dale's for a second.

Gavin laughed.

Everyone had their price, he thought to himself.

"Well there you have it, I guess she's not for sale. So you have one fucking choice. What's it going to be?"

Dale stared over at the young Czech girl once again.

He was nervous.

Gavin had showed a side no one had seen before and his hatred could be felt throughout the room.

"Let me think about it," he uttered getting up and heading towards the bathroom.

"Where the fuck are you going?"

"I gotta use the john man."

"What, did you shit yourself?"

"Jesus! What's your deal? No one told me that you were such an ass."

Gavin smiled.

"What do they say about me?"

Dale hesitated to answer this.

He measured his words carefully as a lot rested on them.

"That you've got the best girls and to bring cash."

"Is that it?"

Dale mustered a smile.

"That you even sold your own girlfriend."

The tension shot high.

With this Dale headed to the bathroom, grabbing the paper as he did.

Gavin headed towards the bar, with Simona following quickly.

"What the fuck Gavin!? You're an ass!"

He didn't say anything.

"Seriously, that was fucked up!"

"Simona. I don't fucking care. I don't give a shit about you. Think about it baby, if I could sell Katka, I could give you away."

She was stunned, hurt.

"Fuck you Gavin!"

"Fuck you too baby."

There was silence.

"Fucking shit! I don't know why i'm here!" Gavin finally said pouring a very stiff drink

"Think of all the money you've made."

He shook his head at this thought.

"There's other things besides money."

She laughed.

"Really, what?"

He wasn't going to say it, as he knew that's what she wanted him to say so that she could pounce all over him, and make him feel worse than he currently felt.

And really what could he say?

"Well, that's a first from you."

They stared hard at one another. Gavin downed his drink and poured another one.

Simona looked carefully at the bottle, it was almost empty.

"You're really hitting it hard today aren't you?"

"I have too."

With this he looked back at Simona, who seemed completely calm, almost bored.

"You're not even affected by any of this are you?"

"Honestly, no. And it wouldn't affect you either if Meeka wasn't murdered."

"I told you not to say that name! Jesus Simona, you're a bitch!"

"Oh come on Gavin! Meeka is not our fault!"

Gavin didn't say anything, but instead looked very troubled by the conversation.

"Every one of these girls had a choice. Most of these girls are getting better lives than they would living here. That's why they went. We didn't force them."

"We?" asked Gavin.

"Yes we, Gavin! Just because you refused to know the girls you were selling doesn't mean it was just me. It's you who scheduled all the meetings. You're the one they call! The one they trust, the girls and the money! After your performance that first time, you put yourself in a whole other league."

Gavin downed his drink then reached for the bottle.

He was so drunk that "first time" that it really was more of getting caught up in the moment and something Gavin didn't really think was going to happen, or was real.

It just happened.

After all, it wasn't his idea to go to the hotel that night.

"The girls saw a guy who could hook them up with a Prince, and the American men saw a guy they could trust and who attracted the best ass in town. Katka was envied by all the girls here for the life she was getting and the men back in the States saw a glimpse of what they could have."

Still he said nothing.

There was a long silence.

"It's just business!" Simona said firmly grabbing the bottle.

Gavin brushed her off.

"Just business?"

"Yes. We supply a service. A service that other people would gladly step into if we weren't doing it. Why shouldn't we make money, and lots of it!"

The words sat in the air.

There had been a lot of money.

The lifestyle had been infectious.

The worse drug you could ever get addicted too.

"...and please, spare me. You know that we wouldn't be having this conversation if Meeka was still alive!"

Gavin looked directly at her, staring her down.

"It started way before Meeka."

Simona smiled, a lascivious smile, that quickly turned even more vile.

"Well Gavin, you're the one that sold your very own girlfriend!"

A dagger to the heart.

"And just in case you forgot, that wasn't just last week!" Simona added twisting the knife. "So fucking spare me!"

Barely audible Gavin responded, "It wasn't supposed to go down like that."

Again silence.

Simona grabbed a bottle of Absinthe from the bar, poured a shot, and drank it down.

The sting and burn apparently having no affect on her at all, as her face remained the same.

"Are you certain of that?"

He wasn't certain of anything anymore. Each week had brought more and more confusion, despair, doubt.

"And as for Meeka, you didn't even know she was one of ours, and wouldn't have if Pat didn't say something."

Unfortunately, this was true.

His friend Pat had told him one morning, when he came busting into his room holding a newspaper completely distraught.

"Tell me, please tell me that you didn't have anything to do with this?" he pleaded throwing the newspaper down on Gavin's bed. There on the front page was an article in the New York Times about a girl who was found stabbed to death. She was from Prague. The article said that she had been a dancer at one of the Gentlemen's clubs. There were no leads at this time.

"Well do you?"

"Do I what Pat?" Gavin asked continuing to read the article.

"Do you know her? Did you have anything to do with this?"

"My girls don't work in strip clubs."

"Oh man, you are not that stupid! You're not that fucking blind are you? Are you!?"

Gavin didn't answer. He was stunned and his mind began to race.

"You know who that girl is don't you?"

"I don't recognize the name."

"So you don't even know the girls you are selling! Wow! Why's that Gavin? Feel a bit guilty?"

Again, no answer.

"Well, the sad thing is, you do know that girl. Remember the really cute brunette who use to come in and say, 'What's up man? or 'You set em up, and i'll knock em down!'?"

Gavin's face turned bleak. Visions of this gorgeous young girl coming in the bar and saying all these funny "Americanisms" ran rampant in his head.

He also recalled the time when he was caught in a rain storm and Meeka ended up sharing her umbrella with him on the steps of Old Town for something like two hours. They sat there laughing and telling stories of their families. She had a younger brother that she was trying to help take care of because her parents weren't doing too good. She just wanted him to have a chance at a better life.

A tear formed in Gavin's eye as he could see her clearly now.

How did she end up in a strip club?

"Jesus man, what have you done?" Pat asked turning to go. As he did so, Simona came walking in from the bathroom.

She had heard everything.

He just looked up at her.

"What?" she asked as if Pat had been talking about nothing important.

"Is she one of ours?" Gavin asked not really wanting to hear the answer.

Simona sat quiet.

"Is she?!"

"….yes."

"That's it. We're finished!"

"What?! We can't!"

"Simona, someone is dead. That could have been Katka. I can't do this anymore. Why didn't you tell me Meeka was one of them? I knew her."

"You've known all the girls."

Gavin's face went white.

"What?"

Gavin collapsed back into bed, turning to face away from Simona.

"How did she end up in a Strip Club?"

There was no answer.

He thought back to that night at the Hotel Inter-Continental. It couldn't have been just a coincidence that they partied there that weekend. Simona knew what she was doing, she must have had a plan.

The real question was did Katka know about it? She had too, Simona was her best friend.
But why would Katka have wanted to go that night?
Why?
Why?

About two weeks after being in Prague, Gavin woke up one morning, completely hung-over and told himself that today was the day he was going to talk to her.
He had confidence on this day. Fueled by the combination of lots of alcohol, little sleep, and an ass that you could bounce a quarter off of that was laying next to him from the night before, Gavin jumped out of bed, splashed some water on his face, threw on some clothes and headed out for coffee.
He hoped she would be there.
She was.
Just as he was walking in, so was she from the other door.
Their eyes met.
She smiled, as did he.
That seemed to say it all.
"Ladies first," he said talking to her for the first time.
She continued to smile and stare at him.
"Thank you," she said in Czech.
"You're welcome," Gavin replied back also in Czech.
This seemed to shock her. Her smile got even bigger, even more beautiful. Something Gavin didn't think was possible.
Then she said something else in Czech. Something that made her eyes sparkle and Gavin blush, even though he had no idea what she said.
It was the way she said it.
It caused the hairs on his arm to stand up.
A jolt shot through his body.

"I'm sorry, I don't speak much Czech."

She mocked frowned.

"That's too bad."

Yes it was, Gavin thought to himself wondering what she had said.

His body was still tingling.

"I've wanted to say hi to you for awhile."

She smiled.

"I've wanted you to say hi to me for awhile."

He blushed.

"Hi," she then said like a smartass.

"Hi," Gavin replied with a smile.

"Finally! Took you long enough!"

Gavin blushed, as this made him feel awesome, and a bit stupid at the same time.

"I'm Katka."

"I'm Gavin."

They shook hands.

"I get your coffee," she said turning to order.

"No, you don't have to do that. Let me."

"No," she said pausing and looking him up and down, "You can get me a drink."

"When?" he said a bit too excited.

She smiled.

That was cute, she thought.

"Well, it looks like you could use one, so how about today at noon?"

"Noon?"

She nodded.

"Yes. Now you can go home and get some sleep," she said with a big smile.

How did she know, Gavin thought.

He smiled.

"Where?"

"St. Nicks."

His favorite bar.

"I see you then," she said grabbing her coffee and beginning to head out.

"Yes," Gavin said a bit startled taking his coffee and just standing there. He felt like he had just won the lottery and still couldn't put it in perspective.

"Good."

Then she turned to walk away stopping just before the door, where she pivoted to face Gavin who was watching her every step.

They shared a moment.

A once in the lifetime kind of moment.

She walked back towards him and stood there for what seemed to be hours.

"I like breakfast better. Do you have plans?"

He smiled.

"I was just going back to bed."

She smiled.

"Well, we should at least have one drink before we do that," she responded biting her lower lip and staring deep into his eyes.

"...if we have too," Gavin added feeling this amazing sexual energy between the two.

Her eyes lit up.

"You sure you don't speak Czech?" she asked in reference to what she had said earlier.

"No, but God I wish I did," Gavin answered staring at her in awe.

"Me too."

This drew huge smiles from the both of them.

They spent the entire day together, lost in conversation and each other's eyes.

"Gavin why are you here in Prague?" Katka asked as they were walking along one of the cobblestone streets.

The question seemed to be one that Gavin didn't like answering, and one that caused a bit of duress.

"I just wanted to get away for awhile," he finally answered.

"From?"

"Life."

It was the way he said it.

"Is everything okay?"

"Yeah, just every now and then you need to take a step back and reevaluate things."

She just listened.

"I just couldn't stay there."

Thinking about it made Gavin angry, very angry. He had done everything by the book, had gone to college, gotten a degree and a job right out of University. One complete with benefits, a matching 401k, everything. Perhaps it was a life that he never really wanted, but still, his parents had been so proud. He never saw it coming.

Sometimes life just isn't fair.

"Why Prague?"

"To find you," Gavin answered with a smile.

They both laughed.

"No, my buddy Pat lives out here and told me to come out and that I could work at his bar. He's been out here for awhile now and loves it, so I figured why not."

"Do you like it?"

"I love it, especially right at this moment."

It was cheesy, but the right thing to say at the time.

Katka loved it.

They stopped walking and turned to one another.

They stared deep into one another's eyes.

"You're absolutely stunning," he said pushing a piece of hair out of her face.

She blushed.

Then they kissed. The kind of kiss that moves mountains, creates dreams.

Writes a fairy tale.

For the next few hours it seemed like they couldn't do anything but kiss, and touch one another.

They couldn't be close enough to one another.

One of those rare moments where the words, "I love you" almost comes rolling off your tongue, but then you realize that you've known one another for less than a day, and don't won't to freak anyone out.

But maybe you wouldn't be?

The entire day this thought danced in his head.

And it seemed that maybe he wasn't alone in his thinking.

Later that night they found themselves back at Gavin's apartment.

"Want a drink baby?" she asked him starting to open the bottle of wine they had bought earlier in the day at a street fair.

"Yeah, that would be great," Gavin answered heading to the bathroom to relieve himself.

She had just called him "baby", he loved that.

He stood there thinking that perhaps his luck had changed.

Could it get any better?

As he came out of the toilet and into his bedroom, Katka stood right before him wearing nothing except for her knee high leather boots.

That answered that.

"Wow...!" Gavin said aloud looking at the most perfect body he'd ever seen.

Katka took the bottle of red and began pouring it down her neck and chest.

"Come get your drink."

"Baby I don't mean it like that," Gavin said pleading to Katka, trying to fix what he obviously had really just fucked up.

Still she said nothing.

The look on her face was one that you would find at a funeral.

She couldn't believe that he was even thinking about this.

Yes, she was all for them giving it a go. And yes she was to blame for them being there as she had agreed with Simona that Gavin was the perfect front man, but this she couldn't see coming.

It wasn't supposed to go down like this.

Was this a test?

Was he serious?

She felt her heart tremble and didn't know what to say.

"Baby, please," he kept saying.

A tear cascaded down her cheek.

"…the guy seems like a very nice man."

Was she really hearing this?

How did they get here?

What a huge mistake she had made.

"Baby, I got a plan."

"Well tell me all about him," Simona said pleading to Katka. "I mean I don't even see you anymore, so who is this guy?"

Katka smiled.

"He's awesome, amazing. Just the nicest guy."

"Yeah, and he's fucking hot too."

Katka smiled.

"And he's American?"

Katka nodded her head in agreement.

"Damn you! You always get the good ones."

"I'm lucky for this one."

"God, and I saw him first!" she said with a hint of jealousy that would only get worse.

"Huh? When?"

"You remember when I told you about that hot American guy that came into the club with Pat a couple of weeks ago? The guy that all the girls went crazy for?"

Katka couldn't remember. Simona was always talking about this guy and that guy. It was impossible to keep track.

"Not really."

"Well I did. I remember him because I guess he's one of Pat's best friends and he just got here."

"Whose Pat again?"

"That rich American guy who owns Marquis de Sade. Anyway, they dropped a bunch of money that night and all the girls kept talking about them. I guess it was one of his first nights here."

"Oh. So he was at the club?"

"Yes. And they seemed to be having a great time."

This seemed to bother Katka a bit.

"Did you dance for him?"

Simona smiled.

"What do you think?"

"Probably."

"Kat, if I had danced for him, he would be with me now!"

"Oh, is that right?!"

Simona smiled.

"You can bet on it."

Katka shook her head.

She didn't like that comment.

"Maybe he doesn't like dancers."

"Wow, that's a low blow!"

"You never know."

"You think he can just be with one girl? A guy like that?"

"What does that mean?"

"You know, he's good looking, young, American."

"And?" Katka said waiting for a point.

"Kat, how many young American guys have you seen come over here and take someone home? They come to party, and hook up with girls."

This irritated Katka, Simona could tell and backed off for a moment.

Just a moment.

"So you think he's different?"

"I think so. He comes from a good family, parents that have been together for thirty five years."

Simona smiled.

"Do you wanna bet?"

"Stop Simona! I think he's different."

There was a long silence. Simona seemed to study Katka for how she might react to her next question.

"I have a more important question to ask you."

Katka got uncomfortable, as Simona's tone changed greatly.

And with Simona you never knew what was coming.

It could be anything.

"What's that Simona?" she asked with trepidation.

"Do you think he would be interested helping out with that idea I was talking to you about?"

"The mail order bride business?"

"Yes."

"Simona! What? Why?!"

"He's a perfect face man."

Katka didn't say anything.

"Think about it. He carries himself well. He's good looking, all the girls love him. Plus the American customers are getting very hesitant in dealing with some of the Czech guys. They are starting to look elsewhere! And they won't trust just me!"

"So?"

"So? So, it's good money, and i'll split it with you!"

These last words hung in the air, definitely catching Katka's attention.

Simona could see this.

"You know your family could use the money."

Again Katka didn't say anything.

This last statement was an understatement.

The money would be very helpful.

"He doesn't really have to do anything, except be a face."

"I don't know Simona."

"Think about it, and think of the money. I'm sure Gavin wouldn't mind putting some dollars in his pocket as well for really doing nothing more than smiling and looking good."

"He does do that very well."

They both laughed.

Katka thought maybe Gavin would even take her somewhere. Maybe back to the States!

She really wanted to get out of Prague.

But then Katka turned back to being more serious.

"I don't know if money is that important to him."

"It is for everyone. Love and money, the two most important things to people, which one would you choose first?"

Katka didn't answer.

This last statement caused a bit of silence until Simona broke it.

"So, he must be rich?" Simona asked.

"I have no idea, but I mean he graduated college and lives in San Francisco which is pretty damn expensive from what I hear. So he must be. But honestly, that's not important."

Simona shot her a disbelieving look.

"Seriously," Katka added.

They both laughed and shot each other looks.

"You must really like him then?"

"More than like. He's amazing."

Simona smiled a very lascivious smile, making Katka blush.

"And yes, in that way too!"

"I knew it! He has that look."

"It's more than a look."

With this they both opened their mouths in mock excitement.

"How long is he staying over here?"

"I don't know, but I don't think it matters."

"Why's that?"

"It's the way he looks at me, I can't explain it, but it fills me with such warmth and happiness that I feel like passing out. It's like our eyes make this pact to never separate."

These last words seemed to upset Simona, stoking her jealousy even more.

They all wanted to find a Prince.

Maybe, just maybe this one was the real deal.

"I'm happy for you," Simona responded without emotion.

She had always wanted what Katka had.

"Thank you."

"So he only has eyes for you?"

"I hope so."

Simona thought about this, and seemed to be scheming in her head.

"I hope so too! But I guess we'll see. And if not?"

Katka shrugged, she didn't even want to entertain this thought.

Gavin had captured her heart and soul.

They were quiet for awhile, Simona had made her point, and wanted to lighten things up.

"Now, let's get back to the more important stuff."

They both smiled very wide, as they both knew what that meant.

"What do you want to know?"

Simona made a measuring motion with her hands.

"Keep going," Katka said with a huge blush.

"No!"

Gavin's mind raced with thoughts of Meeka as well as that night at the Hotel Inter-Continental.

He remembered now that Meeka had been there that night. She had been the one sitting on his knee, acting like she was riding a horse, or maybe it was him!

It teetered back and forth between cute and sexy.

Katka had told him that she was the sweetest thing and that she deserved a break in life.

It had been a rough life, but she never complained.

She just played the hand she was dealt.

Katka had watched over her for the past couple of years as their families were close.

She too loved Katka, and would do anything for her. Katka was like a big sister.

This was all Gavin could think about.

He was in a complete trance and didn't even hear Simona. She had to shake him out of it.

"Gavin, if you're so bothered by Meeka's death. Why'd you set this up?"

He didn't answer.

"Why?"

He didn't want to admit why. He was ashamed.

Gavin thought back to his last phone conversation with Sal, where Sal told him, "This next guy will pay even more. He understands the severity of what happened. You can count on another twenty-thousand easy."

The last few words continued to echo in his mind, over and over.

another twenty-thousand easy…another twenty-thousand easy….another twenty-thousand easy….another twenty-thousand easy

"Huh Gavin, why?" Simona continued to ask.

Gavin shook his head in anger, humiliation, and hatred towards himself.

How much money would be enough to forget?

How much money would be enough to return home and make everything right?

Could he ever make things right?

Why didn't he ever tell Katka?

Would anyone still love him for the things he had done?

"We should get out of here," he finally said.

"No way! This guy is primed and ready to go."

Gavin shot her a look of bewilderment.

Was she crazy?

Did she really not care?

"You need to relax," Simona added coming behind Gavin and putting her arms around him, then lowering them to his pants.

"Let me help you," she said unbuttoning his jeans, "This seemed to help last time."

It had been a week after Katka had gotten on the plane and flew out of his life.

He hadn't heard from her as was the "plan" and he was a complete wreck.

It was all too surreal.

What had happened?

He had essentially been on a bender every since.

So it wasn't that hard for Simona to finally catch up to him.

"Why haven't you returned my calls?" she asked sitting next to him.

He didn't answer.

"Huh Gavin?"

Still nothing.

She shook her head in frustration.

"Have you spent any of the money?"

He turned towards her, as he couldn't believe she was asking this. Nothing about Katka, just the money.

"Have you heard from Katka?" he asked her.

"No."

"Do you know how to get a hold of her?" he asked almost desperately.

"She's gone Gavin. Move on."

"Wow…" Gavin said trailing off and looking away. "That's all you say, move on."

He ordered another drink.

"You need to get your shit together and forget about Katka."

"You say that like it's that easy."

"It is," she said bluntly.

He laughed.

This caused her to smile.

"Gavin, give me a break. She wasn't even the last girl you had sex with, if you remember?"

Her smile turned evil, wicked.

It spoke volumes.

He remembered.

A night like that you never forget.

"Forget about her!"

"I can't."

"Well Gavin, you set that meeting up! Not me! Not anyone else!"

"No, you made us go! It was your idea to go to the Hotel!"

"Ask me something Gavin."

"Huh? What are you talking about?"

"Ask me whose idea it was?"

His heart dropped.

"Fuck you Simona! No way! It couldn't have been."

"Then ask me? But remember, don't ask questions in which you're not prepared to hear the answers."

He was destroyed.

"Why do you think she brought you to the strip club that night? Then to the "party" afterward?"

What the fuck was she saying?

This couldn't be true, could it?

"Just leave me the fuck alone Simona."

"I can't. I need you, and you need me."

"What are you fucking high?"

"We have business you and me, now let's get out of here and get you cleaned up and spend some of the money."

Gavin was flabergasted.

"Simona, what the fuck? She was your friend."

"Yes Gavin she was my best friend, and I couldn't be happier for her to get out of here."

"What about me?"

"What about you Gavin?"

"I loved her."

She smiled.

"Sure Gavin, I could tell. I think it was when your dick was up Nina's ass that the point really hit home."

What could he say to this?

Maybe things had gone a little too far.

"I'm serious Simona."

"Gavin no offense, but come on now. How long did you even know her? Huh? Did you know her?"

He paused before answering, "Yes."

"Really? Did you know that her brother died a few months ago? Huh? Did you know that? Did you know that her family all lives in a one bedroom apartment in Ziskoff? Aunt and Grandma included."

He didn't know any of this.

She kept pounding at him. He kept answering no, no, no.

He was starting to wonder what he did know.

"Gavin, you two had a lot of fun, partied a lot, and had great sex. But come on Gavin, you of all people should know that sex isn't love."

Gavin didn't say anything.

Hadn't it been more than that?

It had to have been.

Katka had said so herself.

But then why?

"Still Simona, we had something."

"If you did, then where is she? Why hasn't she called you?"

Gavin didn't know. He had no idea.

Not knowing killed him.

"And Gavin, why do you think the night before she stayed out with me?"

Gavin's blood raced.

She was talking about the guys from New York, that they had met the night before.

A night that angered Gavin, and had left a lot of unanswered questions.

He felt so uncomfortable about that night.

Just thinking about that night angered him to the deepest levels.

"What happened that night Simona?"

She smiled.

"Tell me."

She shook her head.

"It's not my place to tell you Gavin."

"Please."

He had to know, maybe it would make things better.

Simona sensed this, used this.

"And if you remember, you're the one who brought Katka into it. You two cooked that one up!"

This killed him as this was partially true.

He tried to remember back to their conversation, what had gone wrong, what had happened.

He couldn't.

"Here's what I will do Gavin. I will give you the number of where she's at. You call her, see what she says."

With that she scribbled down the number and began to walk off.

"Good luck Gavin."

Gavin reached down and grabbed the number.

Almost as if it was his salvation.

He began to cry as he clutched the number in his fist.

"Gavin, one more thing," she said pausing at the door, "Sal seemed like a very nice guy, he'll take care of her, and her family." She paused for what seemed to be an eternity until she finally asked, "Will you?"

Then she was gone.

He ordered another drink, and then another one.

The number stayed clutched in his hand.

His knuckles began to turn white.

A tear fell onto the bar.

Gavin was drunk, very drunk.

He opened his fist and let the crumpled number fall on his nightstand. Carefully he unwrapped it so that he could see the number.

He just stared at it.

He thought about all the great times they had spent together. There had been so many.

Then he thought about that smile.

God that smile.

He wondered if she was smiling now?

And then he thought about what Simona had said, and he asked himself, "Will I?"

Will I?

"Did I take care of those clients as I promised I would?"

Slowly he dialed the number.

The phone rang on the other end.

Quickly it was picked up.

"Hello. Hello…Gavin! Is that you, please tell me that's you…"

One of the greatest moments Gavin and Katka had ever spent together was one day when the rain was coming down pretty hard.

Really hard.

The windows were open to Gavin's flat, and they just laid in bed watching the rain.

Listening to the pitter patter of God's tears.

The smell of a fresh rain.

They didn't say much to one another that day, as they didn't have too.

It was the lack of words that said it all.

The silence, and the comfort that they didn't have to say anything, and could just lay there with one another was more than most people would ever experience.

Really it was the sound of two people so connected that just being together was living a lifetime of memories.

It was also the only day that Gavin didn't think about anything from back home, didn't think about anything really at all.

He was just happy.

Truly happy.

He just let himself be and slowly twirled Katka's hair and rubbed her back off and on in between sleeping.

They didn't leave the bed for the entire day.

It was his favorite day.

It was another grey day, and Gavin found himself sitting at the park staring at the Vtlava River. He recalled the last time he was staring at the river when Sal first approached him. He felt similar now.

Confused.

The phone call hadn't gone as planned and he thought about what Simona had talked to him about.

Before he knew it, Simona was upon him as he had called her to meet up.

She came and sat next to him and didn't say anything for awhile.

She seemed rather pleased with herself.

"Now come on now. I will take you shopping. Let's get you some nice suits."

"Suits?"

"Yes Gavin, clothes make the man."

He laughed, but two hours later after being fitted for a couple of pinstripe Armanis, and looking at himself in the mirror looking like a model out of the GQ pages, he started to wonder.

There was power in a nice suit.

"You look hot," Simona said sipping on Champagne as she picked out different accompanying dress shirts and ties.

He felt hot.

Simona could see this.

She added to the fire.

"Gavin you walk in a room like that and you command a presence."

"Thank you."

She smiled.

"Now, one last detail," she said standing up and walking over to him. She reached into her bag and pulled out a box. She opened it and took out a watch.

"Wow!" Gavin said as she put it around his wrist.

A Rolex, with Diamonds, but one that wasn't too over the top, but still one that made one notice.

"Simona, I can't take this."

"Yes you can, and you will."

He hated to admit that he loved it, and wanted to take it off so badly, but he couldn't.

It was a great finishing touch.

It tied everything together, and Gavin started to think that this is what it must have felt like to be one of the partners at the firm he had worked at.

He always had admired their suits, watches, shoes, Porsches, Ferraris. The list went on and on, as money seemed to be able to buy happiness in his old world.

Maybe it could in his new one?

Gavin had that look now, and thirty thousand dollars in his pocket, he actually felt a rush come over him, like one feels when they first do a line of cocaine.

Invincible.

Ready to take on the world.

"Now, let's get some dinner."

"Okay," Gavin said looking at himself in the mirror.

He looked sharp.

Real sharp.

Five minutes later Simona and him walked into one of the most exclusive restaurants in town.

Simona was right, everyone took notice of him.

Girls and guys a like.

Accompanied with Simona, they walked through the crowd of people at the bar, then through the restaurant with all eyes on them.

They were that couple that you see every now and then and you wonder, "Wow! Look at them, what's their life like?"

It was like that night at the Hotel Inter-Continental.

But this time he knew what he was getting himself into.

Or so he thought.

Katka and Gavin had been out drinking one night when they decided to stop by Goldfingers to visit her friend Simona. Gavin was surprised that Katka wanted to take him to a strip club but she responded that, "You can learn a lot about a guy by watching him at a strip club."

He found that interesting.

"You sure it's not to try and make up for last night?"

Katka frowned.

"No, come on Gavin, I thought we were moving on from that?"

Gavin smiled.

It had only happened less than twenty four hours before.

"Sure."

He was still pretty upset at what had transpired the night before. He couldn't believe how Katka had acted with those guys from New York. It was the first time where he actually had started to doubt Katka, or her intentions. So for him this night he was going to take it deep.

It was going to be aggressive.

This turned out to be a huge understatement.

Katka also had to see for herself what Gavin would think about her and Simona's conversation about being a face man. She had wanted to talk with him about this privately but the opportunity hadn't presented itself, and especially given what had happened the night before, she didn't really think it too appropriate.

Yet, she knew Simona had every intention of heading to the hotel after she was off, and she wanted Gavin to come with.

The timing was not good.

"You sure baby?" he asked as they were walking in.

"Yes, I told Simona we would come by."

The strip club was a very decadent place with an Old European theater feel to it. They made their way through the maze of people with Katka saying hello to many of them, and many more of the girls staring at Gavin and smiling. Finally they found a table near the front and Katka slid her chair up next to his. She then motioned over to what had to be one of the most erotic looking girls walking Prague's streets.

It was Simona.

She walked over, blowing off hundreds of guys, with a wave of her hand, like a Typhoon racing through the water.

Her body was built for sin.

She knew it.

She owned it.

"Hi you two," she said putting her hands on Gavin's shoulders briefly as she leaned in to hug and kiss Katka.

Wow, Gavin thought to himself. She looked especially hot tonight. They both were. Every guy in the place looked over at Gavin, all probably wondering who the hell he was.

It felt great.

"Hello Simona."

"Hi Gavin."

She eyed him in such a way that he felt dirty.

It was hot.

He remembered the first time he met Simona. They were all at a club and had been dancing for a number of hours on Ecstacy, when all of a sudden Simona said she had to go. Gavin asked her why and she simply said, "Baby, I gotta get fucked. And Katka doesn't want to share you, which is really, really too bad."

He was floored.

Yes, it really was too bad.

Later that night Katka asked him if he wanted to fuck her, and he told her, "Just you baby, and only you…"

"Promise?"

"Promise."

Tonight was a new day.

He was still really upset at Katka from the night before.

"Shall I dance?" Simona asked.

"But of course."

For the next hour or so Simona danced. Every now and then stopping to make out with Katka and tell her how beautiful she was. She had always loved Katka, sometimes too much.

Simona also waived over several other girls to introduce to Gavin. Each one of them truly stunning and loving that he was American.

Some had remembered him from the first time and had heard a lot about him from both Katka and Simona.

They were all impressed.

He had this aura about him, that many found enticing, almost irresistible, especially because he didn't take himself so seriously and was just fun to be around.

Gavin thought it was simply the power the American Passport had over there.

Many of the girls asked him about America and from Gavin's perspective it appeared that they all thought all Americans lived like Beverly Hills 90210 characters.

Maybe because his friend Pat's life was very similar to that, and Pat was a frequent patron.

Gavin laughed and did little to debunk this stereotype.

"Simona, now do only him," Katka said later in the night wanting to watch Simona dance for Gavin.

She was going to let out the leash, and see how far Gavin would take it, as the entire night he seemed to be…well different.

"I would love too!" she said licking her lips.

Simona danced on and for Gavin so sexually that when she grinded on him, it was obvious he was hard. She then whispered in his ear, "I'd let you stick that anywhere."

"Oh my God," Gavin said aloud.

Katka smiled, but not the same smile she always smiled.

This one was different, almost forced and her eyes seemed to be studying and measuring him up.

Gavin caught this, but at this point was so drunk and intoxicated by Simona and the other girl's bodies that he didn't labor on it too much.

Plus, he still had the images of the guys from New York.

Fuckers.

After a few more hours, Simona finally got off, and they all headed out. She invited out six other girls and said she knew of a party over at the Hotel Inter-Continental, where apparently she also had a suite reserved.

Gavin was pretty drunk and kind of wanted to go home, but was on a mission this night given what had happened. Plus, one just doesn't turn down the invitation to party at the Hotel Inter-Continental with eight jaw dropping beauties that had bodies sculpted by God himself, and the desire to "Drink and fuck all night" as Simona shouted as they jumped in a cab.

If him and Katka had only just gone home.

It had been a few days after Gavin had talked with Simona about moving forward, and Gavin wanted to talk to Pat about it. He knew what Pat would say, but hoped maybe he would be surprised.

He wasn't.

"You're kidding me right?" Pat asked Gavin.

Gavin shook his head, "No, i'm serious."

Pat was stunned.

"Dude, nothing good can come out of this."

"I can make some money."

"So."

"So?"

"Yeah."

"So, I don't have any money! I'm fucking broke and I could really use it. Fuck man, you know what happened? I've got fucking legal bills."

Pat was quiet, trying to choose his words. This was a very sensitive topic and he had to measure his words carefully. No one really knew what to say after it happened, and everyone had been walking on eggshells on this topic.

"There has to be another way."

"I wish there was."

There was a long silence before either of them said another word.

"Believe me Pat, I wish there was another way, and it's not like this is illegal, it's just business over here."

This was a valid point.

And the one that Gavin clung too.

"Dude, what would your mother think?"

Gavin threw his arms up in the air.

"Probably not much less than she already does now."

The pain was written all over his face and he looked like a desperate man.

Pat didn't know what to say. He knew Gavin's parents and how it tore him up.

"I'm trying man," Gavin said with the voice of a broken man.

Then he walked off.

Pat stood there watching him, thinking back to the Gavin he knew in college.

He didn't know this man now.

But how could he fault him?

What could he say?

Nine months earlier, about a month after Katka left, Gavin found himself smoking a cigarette and having a drink waiting for his "appointment".

This would be the first one.

Scheduled one that is.

He had decided to go through with the business, as he never heard from Katka, only Sal, and Simona had been way too convincing. She had made him feel like Katka and him weren't anything special, though he still battled with it intensely.

Maybe it was his ego?

Or all the money, the clothes, the life.

Truthfully, he loved that part.

It was intoxicating.

They had spent almost every dime of what they had made in the Katka deal, and it had felt good.

Real good.

He figured he would just do these two, and that was it.

In and out.

Then get out of Prague.

Start over.

As he was sitting there waiting he began to get a bit nervous as he wasn't really too sure what he was doing. He caught a glimpse of himself in the mirror.

He looked panicked so he headed over to the bar to get a quick shot to calm his nerves. As he did so he caught the attention of a few very good looking girls who were sitting belly up. They looked him up and down and smiled.

That's all he needed.

That was his shot.

He smiled over at the two and they waived for him to come over. He shook his head politely and said that he couldn't, not now.

He had business.

They mock frowned.

"Later," he said turning to walk back into the lobby with a little zest in his step.

The same lobby he had walked into about a month before that night with Katka, Simona and a few other girls.

He couldn't help but think about that night, that weekend.

Life changing.

Gavin remembered walking through the doors that night into this amazingly beautiful Hotel lobby, with marble floors, columns, chandeliers with a thousand bulbs, and a ceiling that seemed to go to the moon.

It looked like a museum.

It was packed and everyone of the people seemed to stare at Gavin as soon as he walked through the revolving doors.

Like a rock star taking the stage of a sold out show.

Granted, it was most likely because he was flanked by Katka and Simona with six other girls almost falling over him.

He was like a modern day Hugh Hefner, without the smoking jacket.

All eyes were on them and continued to be as they found a few chairs at the bar and continued to party as if it was New Years.

Guys especially seemed to be entralled by Gavin with many of them coming up to him and introducing themselves.

Gavin had no idea why, but loved the attention and ordered drinks for everyone.

Every now and then he would catch Simona sitting with a few of the guys, occasionally pointing over to Gavin and waving.

Gavin would wave back and smile, asking Katka, "What is that girl doing?"

Katka laughed and said, "That's just Simona."

He shook his head now as he thought to himself, yeah, that was Simona just laying the groundwork.

He wondered if he had met his "appointment" that night.

That night had been such a blur, as was the following morning when he had gotten caught up with all of it, and…well, his talk with Sal.

He couldn't think about that right now.

Time to focus.

Finally two older men in nice suits, perhaps Brook Brothers came in. Gavin glanced over in their direction.

They walked over, a bit hesitant. They were both dressed very nicely and had that look as though they probably spent most of their nights watching reruns of Murder She Wrote and playing Cribbage.

Cribbage?

Seriously.

"Gavin?"

"Yes, Dick?"

They shook hands.

"Nice to meet you."

"Likewise, and this is Bill."

They also shook hands.

"Please have a seat."

"Here?"

"Yes, is there a problem?"

"I thought we would do this in a little bit more privacy."

"Don't worry, we're just talking right now."

"About what?"

"About you."

"What do you want to know?"

"You guys drink?"

"A little."

"You into weird shit like defecation, golden showers, etc...the like?"

"Excuse me."

"You heard me."

"Listen man, we don't need this shit."

"Then I guess you don't need my girls."

The two were obviously a bit annoyed, and uncomfortable, but neither of them wanted to get up and walk away.

They had traveled way too far and the opportunity to have what Sal had, they would put up with this.

"I play bridge with a foursome and Bill here occasionally likes to dip his cigar in brandy. That's about as wild as we get."

Gavin smiled.

"Well, that's as long as brandy is a drink!"

He then laughed, and nervously, Bill and Dick joined in.

"Not that I wouldn't try that," Gavin added.

They all continued to laugh.

"Anyway, that's more like it. So, why you two?"

"The same as Sal. We're just tired of the game. We just want some companionship."

"Seems to be a lot of tired men your age. You all should get more rest."

"Thanks for the tip."

"You're welcome. Anyway, you have the money?"

"Of course. You have the girls?"

Again Gavin smiled, this time the smile stretched from ear to ear.

"But of course," he said getting up and motioning to the elevator like a Circus Ring Leader.

Once inside Gavin hit the Penthouse Button. He had decided to go all out and really impress his new clients. On the way up, Bill asked Gavin, "So how is it that you get the most beautiful girls?"

Gavin just stared at him, then finally answered.

"Because I do a little more than play bridge and dip my cigar in brandy."

They all laughed.

"I bet it doesn't hurt being a young American, with good looks," Dick added.

"Careful Dick, i'm not an option."

Dick smiled.

It was a little eerie as Gavin thought to himself that this guy could almost definitely be an ass bandit.

"No really, Sal said that your girls blow away the others. Why is that?"

Gavin thought hard about this.

What would allow him to sleep at night?

Then it came to him.

"I deliver the fairy tale, or at least a new version of it."

Simona had told the girls that Gavin could deliver them the world, as he had done for Katka. That's what he was doing.

Right?

Finally the elevator had made it's way up, opening to a long hallway with two oversized doors at the end.

"Gentlemen, this is why you flew ten thousand miles."

They all walked down the hallway, anticipation growing with each step.

Upon opening the doors Dick and Bill's eyes were met with the gaze of eight stunningly beautiful Czech girls dressed in cocktail dresses, sitting about drinking wine. They all smiled lasciviously, creating the mood of a porno about to be shot, with Dick and Bill being the stars.

It was quite the site.

Both guys were taken aback, as was Gavin a bit himself.

"After you," Gavin finally said realizing that everyone was still standing at the door.

The guys walked in and nervously headed over to the couches. Gavin headed over to the bar to make himself a drink. Simona came over to talk to him. She was wearing a dress without a back and very low around her breasts. She looked incredible.

"Very impressive Simona," Gavin said making a waving motion towards the girls, and then to her.

She smiled.

"Thank you. Why didn't you come up earlier?"

"I don't want to know the girls."

"Why?"

"I'm having a hard enough time with the whole Katka affair. It's only been a month."

"Oh, so is that why you're continuing to do business?"

"Fuck off Simona, you're the one who said we should do it."

She smiled.

With this Gavin poured himself a stiff drink, downed it, and poured another.

"Don't hit it too hard."

"Simona, I'm a little on edge. This isn't exactly my specialty!"

"Are you sure about that? You obviously did a pretty damn good job the first time with Katka. Referral business is the best."

"Watch it Simona."

"Gavin, listen there's no need to be like that. I know that you liked Katka very much, but we've talked about this."

Gavin didn't know what to say. He still missed Katka very much.

And now being back in this suite and with the impending business, he was a bit rattled.

"Are you trying to tell me that you wouldn't like a shot at one of these girls," she asked pausing deliberately, so she could lick her lips, touch him on the arm delicately, and then add, "Or me?"

The way she asked felt like foreplay, and Gavin could feel his body reacting.

He froze.

She was intense.

A true force.

Simona smiled, and then continued.

"I'm not trying to be a jerk. I'm just being realistic. You're a good looking young man Gavin, very good looking. And you're young. So was Katka. What happened, happened."

"How can you be so cold about it? She was your best friend!"

"Because I can Gavin! Because I grew up with her and am happy she got out of here! I'm happy she doesn't have to worry about money!"

This hurt.

"You have no idea Gavin! You Americans take everything for granted."

"What about me then Simona? Huh, what about me? I miss her."

"You need to move on."

"And what do you propose?"

To which Simona leaned in.

"After our business is finished with these two guys, just stick around the suite. We do have it for the night and as you know the girls really love to party."

With this last bit, Simona walked behind Gavin and put her hands on Gavin's hips.

"Plus, I know you like things on the wild side! Perhaps a repeat of what happened the first time we were all in here?!"

Gavin didn't say anything, but just kept drinking. His mind was racing with very dirty thoughts.

He was very turned on.

Her hands moved up to Gavin's shoulders.

"You're so tense baby," Simona said massaging Gavin.

"I have a lot on my mind."

With this she quickly slid her hands down Gavin's body to his crotch, unzipped his pants and took him in her hands.

It was so quick and deliberate, he didn't have time to object.

A professional move.

"Let me help you."

"Simona," he said trying desperately not too enjoy how good it felt, "…. don't," the last word barely audible.

"That didn't sound too convincing."

She continued massaging him, as the girls entertained the guys right there in front of him. He stood there watching them all drink and frolic, as his blood boiled, his heart raced.

God it felt good!

Too good.

Faster and faster, tighter and tighter Simona worked her magic, biting and blowing in his ear.

He was about to explode and she sensed it, grabbing it even harder and playing with his balls.

"Fuuuuuuuuuckkkkkk!" he said shooting all over the carpet, as Simona continued to tug at him, slowly, getting each and every drop.

"Oh my God!" he said pushing her off and zipping up. He grabbed a towel from the bar, wiped his forehead, downed a drink and headed over to the party.

He had just been pushed over the edge.

"So, see anything you like?"

"Your girls are stunning!"

"Yes, every one of them is a little slice of heaven."

"And hell I hope!" Gavin added finding a seat next to two of the girls.

The guys didn't answer, no need for one.

Everyone understood what that meant.

"So I assume we're going to continue our business?"

"Yes."

"But I have one concern?"

"What's that Bill?"

"How do you guarantee they don't take off?"

Gavin smiled.

"Take off?"

"Yes, run away."

"Ummm dude, they're not mice!"

Gavin laughed, as did some of the girls.

"No really?" Bill asked.

"Listen this isn't a refrigerator. I can't guarantee shit. What I can tell you though is that as long as you keep a girl happy, you'll do just fine."

"And how do I do this?"

Gavin's smile got bigger, Simona even laughed a bit.

"If you don't know how to do that then I can't help you."

"Seriously?" Bill asked.

"Seriously. Even Cupid can only do so much!"

"He does have a good point there," Dick added trying to keep things jovial.

"Listen, I'm not selling appliances. What do you want?"

Everything went quiet, as this question seemed to head down a road that no one really wanted to go down.

You could feel it.

Finally Bill spoke up.

"How about their parent's addresses and phone numbers?"

Gavin wasn't expecting this.

"What!?"

"...some people do it that way."

Gavin looked stunned, angered, ticked off.

"That's not my style! "

"That's standard for most deals," Bill pushed.

Gavin didn't like the turn this had taken. He shook his head.

"No."

Bill kept pushing, causing Gavin to jump up off the sofa.

Gavin raised his hand up.

"Stop right there, we're not doing that."

Bill kept up the attack.

"Come on man, don't be like that!"

"Yeah, just work with us, we're certainly paying you enough," Dick added.

Gavin shot him a look of surprise.

"It's not about the money."

They both smiled.

"Are you sure about that?" Dick asked.

"Now you've pissed me off! No deal. Get the fuck out of my face!"

This stunned both men and they shared surprised glances.

Dick tried desperately to calm the situation.

"You know that most guys get the addresses so that they can send the parents money. Once the parents get the money, and get used to receiving it, they put pressure on the girls to stay with the guy."

Gavin seemed puzzled.

What was happening here?

"So what you're saying is, you can't do it on your own?"

They shrugged an almost pathetic shrug.

"At our age, we can use every edge we can get. As Dick said, the parent's themselves get used to the money coming in. That's huge for us! Plus, let's be honest right now. We don't look like you, dress like you, or have what you have. That tie alone probably cost more than my entire outfit."

Dick jumped in. "As sad as it is, it's true."

"You guys seem to know quite a lot about this?"

"You would too if you were going to spend forty thousand on a girl to come back over to the States and...," he said pausing to look over at Dick, "Be your wife."

"I mean come on Gavin," Bill added, "That's a normal thing in most of these deals. I'm surprised you haven't dealt with it before," he said as if almost questioning Gavin's experience.

It caused Gavin to pause.

"I'm sorry, but that's not my deal. I thought this was going to go down just like Sal's did."

"It will, it's just...well..."

"We're not as confident as Sal. Sal's situation is a bit different."

"Well that's not my problem guys, but yours. I'm sorry we couldn't do business."

Gavin said the last bit almost a bit relieved.

Actually he was very relieved.

I mean, really, what the fuck was he doing, he thought to himself.

He stood up, headed over to the bar, when all of a sudden a voice spoke up.

"Wait! I can get you their addresses."

Gavin almost stumbled upon hearing this. It was Simona, and she continued, "But for that you pay extra."

"We're paying enough as it is."

"Well then you'll pay more or nothing. It's your decision."

The guys looked at one another.

"You can get us their addresses and numbers?" Dick asked seeking reassurance.

"I'll get you their fucking bios and baby pictures if your little heart so desires, and you pay for it!"

"How much extra?" Bill asked with apprehension.

It was silent until Gavin stepped forward, drink in hand and said with firmness, "Ten thousand!"

He smiled, then added, "Each!"

"That's fucking outrageous!"

"So is your demand!" Gavin fired right back. "Take it or leave it. I'm getting very annoyed. Sal didn't say anything about this."

"Well he doesn't have too. Katka is never without a smile and she's adopted the US like her own."

"Yes, she really does seem to love him," Dick added almost looking at Gavin for a reaction.

He got one, as the mere mention of her name turned Gavin's eyes to ice and his disposition to that of Satan.

Simona noticed and jumped in, "You heard him. Ten extra cash or look somewhere else, and good luck with that. Because the one thing we can guarantee is you will not find better!"

As she said this Bill and Dick looked around to the the eight beauties sitting there. Each one of them stared at them, eyes wide open, mouths half open as if they were inviting oral sex.

The guys turned to one another.

"Can we have a word alone?"

"Of course," Gavin said motioning to one of the bedrooms.

With this Gavin and Simona walked to the other bedroom on the opposite side.

Gavin was irate.

"What the fuck are you thinking volunteering their addresses?"

"Come on Gavin. That's how most agencies do it!"

"How the fuck do you know!?!" Gavin asked completely distressed.

She smiled. Had he forgotten about last month?

"Gavin, it's one of the fastest growing trends in Eastern Europe. It's becoming big business!"

"So!?!? How do you know so much?"

"Because Gavin I have friends, and not all of us are so lucky to have an American passport. Girls would kill for the opportunity to get over there!"

"Still in the US it's looked down upon!"

"Well isn't that a bunch of hypocrisy then?!!"

"Why's that?"

"Because American men are the ones buying up most of the girls!"

She smiled at him.

"Well, we're not a fucking agency! I'm done after this."

"Gavin if you were done with this, you would never have agreed in the first place."

"Don't Simona..."

"Anwyay, you don't care about that. You're just mad about Katka!"

He stared hard at her. He looked as though he was about to burst!

She stared back, almost crazy.

"What do you think she's doing right now? Huh? Huh?!!?" she pushed, and pushed, getting up in his face.

Visions of Katka with Sal started flooding his head.

He couldn't take it.

"Shut up Simona! Shut the fuck up!"

"Come on Gavin….get pissed off. I love it angry!"

With this he snapped and threw her down on the bed, where in one motion he lifted her dress, ripped her underwear and took his cock out.

She was breathing hard, staring at him with daggers.

He rammed it up inside of her, deep and hard.

She sighed almost cried.

"Oh fuck…" she said, gripping him around the back with her legs!

He kept thrusting at her deep and hard.

There was a knock at the door.

"Gavin?"

"What?!" Gavin yelled watching Simona's eyes roll back.

The sounds of sex filled the air.

"…we have a deal."

Gavin smiled, kissed Simona feraciously, then added, "Good. I'm glad we could get over the hump. Let's meet tomorrow to finalize the deal."

"Sounds good."

"Good. Goodnight then. We have booked you two rooms in the hotel."

"Thank you."

"…no, thank you!"

He kissed Simona hard on the mouth again as he thrusted with as much repulsion as he could muster.

A true hate filled fuck.

Things would never be the same.

Exactly what he thought the first time he was in this Hotel.

That night at the Hotel Inter-Continental there had been some crazy partying. The Absinthe had been broken out, coke had been cut, and all morality had been thrown out the window.

It was Soddom and Gomorrha.

Gavin felt like a Rock Star, as the girls were hanging off of him, making him the center of attention.

Katka was crazy that night, a sexual dynamo. It was a side of her he had never seen.

Dangerous. But incredibly sexy.

He didn't know if she was trying to make up for the night before, or what, but everyone was on a different level.

And for some very bizarre reason guys were trying to talk to him all night about "business".

"Business?" Gavin asked laughing, "The only business we have tonight is this," he said putting his hands out to the girls and the environment around him.

One of the guys, had told him that Gavin's girls could make him a lot of money and that he would really like to talk.

Gavin laughed as he thought this guy was ridiculous.

The guy kept talking to him and Gavin had to tell him to fuck off. It was the only downer of the night.

"I just thought you and I could work well together," he said starting to walk off.

"Fucking whack job," Gavin responded turning his attention back to the Motley Crüe after party.

Wait, was that the same guy from earlier he wondered?

The guy at the pisser he had met. At the club.

Then things got real aggressive when they went upstairs to the Suite, for as soon as they walked in most of the girls felt the need to abandon their clothes and boundaries.

With more coke being cut it was inevitable that this would turn out to be an epic night. A night where Gavin found himself on the couch laying back after taking a serious Elvis line, when before he knew it his jeans had been torn open and one of the girls had taken him in her mouth, as another one then turned his face towards hers so she could kiss him on the mouth.

KATKA

He was so fucked up he had no idea whether or not Katka was one of them, and at that moment it didn't matter.

Turned out that she was just the General in the all out assault of Gavin, and the storming of his dick!

The only time that it really crossed his mind is when he found himself standing over another girl who was on all fours with her face buried deep down into Katka, with Katka looking up at him with those eyes.

He had seen eyes like this once before when he was hunting as a kid with his dad. At that time they belonged to a deer they had shot.

Glassy eyed and still.

Dead.

Katka had those eyes now, but at the same time she was telling him, "Come on baby fuck her...give it to her..."

The rest of the night was a complete blur and he woke up the next morning in a luxurious bed laying next to Katka and two other girls.

"Did you have fun last night?" Katka asked putting her head on his chest.

"Yeah, did you?"

She didn't answer.

"Do you think it was too much?"

Gavin laughed.

"Yeah, I would say so. After that i'm never going back home."

She laid there lifeless.

"I'm serious."

"Huh?"

"That was such a fun night."

Katka was about to say something, as she really wanted to talk to Gavin, needed to talk to him, when Simona walked in carrying Mimosas.

It was one of those mornings where there was no option, you needed the hair of the dog just to get through.

They all did.

He couldn't remember if it had been Simona's idea to go downstairs to eat, or whose. He remembered Katka wanting to stay in bed and order room service, and watch movies.

How different things would be if they had done that.

But before he knew it they were all in the elevator heading downstairs, almost as if they were going to repeat the night before, as they were all ripped again and the party was on.

However, when the elevator opened, it wasn't the lobby. The doors opened to what was obviously the Conference room floor, as there were guys and girls standing there almost in anxious anticipation to see who it was. Then when their eyes focused on Gavin and his crew, all of them seemed to be excited and happy.

Gavin thought he recognized some of them, but couldn't be sure.

"What the fuck is this?" he asked taking a step forward, once again flanked by both Katka and Simona.

"Let's check it out," Simona added almost too excited.

All the girls followed and all eyes continued to be glued to them. It was a room of mixed emotions as the guys were excited, the other girls not so much.

They found a group of overstuffed chairs towards the end of the hallway and set up camp.

Gavin had barely sat down when some guy called his name.

"Gavin?"

"…ummm yeah," Gavin said looking up.

"Hey you remember me, we talked last night?"

Gavin laughed, as he had no idea.

"No, i'm sorry…last night was a little…"

The guy smiled, he understood.

"Anyway, I was interested in your services."

"My services?" Gavin asked half joking, the other half having no idea what the fuck this guy was talking about, but he humored him.

"Yes, I was interested in one of your girls."

"Who isn't?" Gavin said looking at the group. They were all gorgeous.

"True," the guy said letting out a little laugh.

"…anyway, what are you looking for?" Gavin asked, again not sure what was going on.

"God, any of your girls would be great."

Gavin smiled. No shit, he thought.

"Yes, they are…"

"Well, what are your prices?"

"What are you looking to spend?" Gavin asked not too quite sure what he was discussing.

"Well most of these outfits are charging about twenty thousand."

"Twenty-thousand!" Gavin thought to himself.

Wow! For what?

What the fuck were they talking about he wondered?

Simona noticed this and jumped in.

"Listen, Meeka why don't you go talk with this man for a minute. Katka and I need to talk to Gavin."

Meeka did just that.

Simona then turned to Gavin, "So, you want to make some money Gavin?"

What would you say?

"What's going on here Simona?"

"Gavin, these gentlemen are here to find wives."

"Excuse me?"

"Yes. You've never heard of mail order brides?"

Gavin laughed.

"Ummm…yes, but never **really** took it too serious."

"Well, it's serious business here, and guys pay big dollars to find girls to come back to the States with them."

Gavin was speechless.

"And we are at one of their conferences now."

"So is that why we came here?"

Simona smiled.

"Yes."

"Really?! Wow! I don't know what to say."

"You don't have to say anything. Just act like you're the man."

"Me? Why me?"

"Because Gavin, you are the all American Man who is surrounded by beautiful girls. You immediately stand out. Look around."

He did so.

"Think back to last night."

Gavin wasn't sure what she was talking about, but he remembered feeling like a rock star the night before.

"Most of these agencies are run by foreigners and some of the American men get a little hesitant, but with you, they see you as one of their own. Plus, look at the other girls."

He did.

They were okay, but just that. The girls he was with that day were the kind that you would cut off your left nutt for.

"I can't do this. I can't do this to one of these girls."

"Gavin, girls want to go over to America! Everyone does. It's the land of opportunity, and for most of these girls life will certainly be better over there."

"Why's that?"

"Gavin, open your eyes. Life is different here. Very different. People see the US as the land of opportunity still, especially girls."

He thought about this.

"Do you want to go?" he asked Simona directly.

"...if i could have someone take care of me...yes."

"And you Katka?"

She smiled at him.

"Would you?" he urged wanting an answer.

She sat quiet for a moment and just stared into his eyes, and then finally answered.

"..with you."

It was as if she wasn't answering the question, but pleading with him, making the question more than just a question.

But he thought about the night with the guys from New York. That's why she paused, in his mind.

What did she really want?

He sat speechless for a minute.

He didn't really know what to think at the moment.

This was crazy, right?

"What do you think baby? Should we do this?" he asked Katka.

"It's up to you Gavin."

Gavin stared hard at her, he couldn't believe what they were talking about. He stood up.

He was pretty fucked up.

"I gotta piss."

And he walked off.

Katka smiled and looked at Simona. She seemed to be happy with Gavin's reaction.

"He didn't say no," Simona said as they both watched Gavin walk off.

As he did so, one of the men decided to follow him.

That man would turn out to be the deciding factor.

But for a very steep price.

The day before the Hotel Inter-Continental night, Gavin had taken a call from home. He didn't say much, just listened, but it was apparent that the conversation wasn't very good.

He hung up the phone slowly, took a deep breath, rubbbed his eyes, then stood up and walked out of his apartment. He was to meet Pat at the corner and then head over to St. Nicks to meet Katka and her friends.

"Hey man," Pat said as Gavin approached.

"What's up?" Gavin answered glumly.

"Whoa man, you alright?"

He wasn't.

This whole thing at home had taken a serious toll on him.

"I need Katka. She always cheers me up."

"Want to talk about it?"

"No, but thank you."

"I'm here for you."

"I know, but I just don't want to discuss it."

Pat didn't either really.

All Gavin wanted was to hold Katka in his arms.

They had become so close that she was his everything, and being around her, everything else seemed to disappear.

She just made it seem as though things would be okay.

When they got to the bar Katka was in the middle of talking to three guys, she didn't even notice when they walked up. This irritated Gavin to no end.

Pat noticed.

The three guys were all cookie cutouts of the same thing; good looking, members of a health club that probably offered Pilates, college educated, and very well dressed.

Loaded as well.

Katka still didn't notice them.

"Holy shit man!" Gavin said to Pat.

"Dude, don't worry."

Finally after about two minutes of standing there, in which Simona had noticed as well, Simona said something.

"Hey Gavin, Pat..."

Katka turned, she looked a little bit hesitant and uneasy of herself.

Simona continued.

"You having a moment there Katka?"

Katka tried ignoring this. However, both Pat and Gavin caught this and both were dumbfounded.

Katka tried to recover.

"Hey baby, you finally made it."

She gave him a big hug.

"Well, perhaps I shouldn't have."

This comment seemed to unsettle everyone.

Katka decided to blow through it.

"Guys, this is my boyfriend Gavin and his friend Pat."

The guys nodded, as guys do when a beautiful girl's boyfriend shows up and their fantasies of taking her home come crashing down.

"Boyfriend?" one of them asked as if he couldn't believe that it could be true from his short time talking with Katka.

A total cock move.

"...oh, well, it's nice to meet you man. And you're American?"

"Yeah."

"Cool. You guys traveling around like us?" he continued referring to his two buddies.

"No, we live here."

"That's very cool."

"You?"

"New York. We're just over here on a little vakay. Market is slow and instead of giving back everything we decided to get out for awhile. And with the month we had last moth....hell, we might stay here as well!" He added banging glasses with his friends.

They all clinked glasses, laughed and guzzled down.

"Oh, you're traders?"

"Yeah. You?"

"Nothing, just bartending over here."

This comment also seemed to resonate throughout. The tension continued to rise.

"I'm going to get a drink. Pat, you want one?"

"Yeah."

"Hey man, we got a tab down. Just put it on ours. It's amazing how cheap it is over here. We could buy drinks for the whole bar and it's not even going to cost near the same that a night out in Manhattan does!"

Gavin smiled after hearing this, turned to Pat and they then turned to the bar and started ordering drinks.

"So Katka, I was saying...I have a lot of connections in New York and LA if you're looking to move over. Plus I own a building in New York if you need a place."

Gavin heard this and was convinced this was more for him than Katka, he was seething at this point.

What the fuck was this about?

Move to New York or LA?

Pat put his hand on his shoulder, "Dude, calm down. It's nothing. Just a guy with no game."

Gavin forced a smile and ordered a Martini.

This went on for awhile, this bravado, it was almost entertaining, but for Gavin also very lame. Katka tried to grab Gavin's hand several times, but he kept pushing her away.

"Hey Gavin, I was telling Simona and Katka that we're heading to Cannes tomorrow. We've rented a yacht. There's plenty of room. The girls seem pretty interested. What do you say?"

"About what?"

"Joining us?"

Gavin turned to Katka, who looked...odd.

Simona jumped in.

"We should go. Chris has offered to buy our tickets."

"I'm outta here," Gavin said on the border of snapping. He put his drink down and like that was on a beeline for the door. Pat chased after him.

"Gavin wait!"

He finally caught up to him.

"You fucking shitting me dude?" Gavin said as Pat came running up. "After the day I've had."

"Hey man..."

"What!?!? What are you going to say? Huh? What!?"

Then Katka came running out.

Finally.

"Gavin!"

Gavin looked at her, then at Pat, and turned to walk away. Katka chased after him.

"Gavin wait!"

She ran up to him and grabbed him, he shrugged her off.

"Gavin why are you leaving?"

"You didn't just ask that did you?"

"Why are you so upset?"

"You don't know?"

"No."

"You don't do you? Holy shit!"

"Oh come on!"

"You know what....fuck it! I'll see you later!"

Gavin walked off and Katka just stood there. He stopped after about fifteen feet. Still facing away from her he asked, "You're not coming are you?"

"I can't leave Simona."

Like a dagger to the heart.

He forced a laugh.

"Of course..."

Then he was gone. Pat turned to Katka and just stared at her, then began shaking his head.

"Of all the days Katka."

"What?"

"He just hasn't had a very good day."

"What happened?"

Pat told her.

"Well, what did I do?"

"Come on now Katka, what's going on in there?" Pat asked nodding to the bar they just left.

"Nothing. Simona just met a few guys that she's interested in."

"Is it just Simona?"

That's all that was said.

Later that night back at Gavin's apartment, Katka walked in. She saw Gavin sitting on the window sill. Gavin didn't say anything.

"Hey you," she said walking up.

Nothing.

"You're mad at me? I don't understand why? What did I do?"

Gavin looked at her and studied her face.

"It's been three hours Katka. Where the fuck have you been?"

"With Simona."

"Just Simona?"

"...and those guys."

"Get the fuck out!"

"What?! Why?!"

"You hung out with those guys all night after it was obvious that I was pissed?"

"You don't trust me?"

"No, I don't think I do."

"Why? I haven't done anything."

"Are you sure?"

"Gavin i'm in love with you."

"So in love with me that you come running after me, three hours later?"

"I told you, I couldn't leave Simona."

"Oh come on! We're talking about Simona, the same girl who takes trips to Budapest and Moscow by herself!"

"We were just talking."

"About what? And for this long? Guys like that don't have anything to talk about this long. You know what time it is?"

"I'm not having this conversation. I love you, and only you. If you don't know that then there's nothing I can do. I don't know what else I can do."

"I don't know. Just showing you care would probably be enough."

"I do care Gavin. I guess I'm just bad at showing it."

"That's too bad."

"Yes, it is."

❖ ❖ ❖

Gavin made his way back down to the lobby, ordered a drink from the bartender and took a seat facing outside to the Vtlava River. It was raining and Gavin allowed his mind to get lost in the scene. It helped, as his mind was racing with all kinds of thoughts and questions.

What were Simona and Katka talking about?

Were they serious?

With what happened the night before was Katka the girl he thought she was?

His mind ran, he didn't even notice the older man approach him from his left.

"Excuse me, Gavin?" the man asked gently, trying to be as courteous as he could.

Gavin didn't hear him the first time.

"Gavin?" the man said once again putting his hand on Gavin's shoulder.

Gavin turned almost violently.

"What the fuck?"

"Sorry about that. I was just hoping I could have a word with you."

"What would you like to talk about?"

The man smiled.

"You have very beautiful girls."

"Thank you."

"I've never seen someone with so many gorgeous women come to one of these."

"And what are you doing here?"

The man smiled a bit and looked down almost as if he were embarassed to admit why.

"Oh."

"I was hoping I could talk to you about one of your women."

"Sure. Please have a seat."

The man sat down.

"My name is Sal."

"I'm Gavin."

They shook hands.

"So you're American?" Sal asked.

"Yes, I am."

"Where you from?"

"Born in Arizona."

"Nice place."

"Yes, if you like the heat."

"What brought you over here?"

Gavin smiled.

"Know anywhere else you can get a beer for thirty cents and a piece of ass like that?" he said motioning back to the room full of girls.

The guy laughed.

"Good point."

There was an uncomfortable silence.

"Anyway, you don't find many Americans in this business."

Gavin didn't say anything to this.

"I like that. I trust that more. Some of these guys are a bit shady and the girls they get are even shaddier."

"I bet."

"But a fellow American, sits better."

"So how do you know i'm not shady?"

"I don't. I just know that Americans understand greed better than anyone."

Gavin found this interesting.

Again he didn't say anything.

"Greed is good."

"What is this Wallstreet?"

The guy laughed.

"No, but it can be."

Sal seemed to measure this, take Gavin in.

"So, why you Sal?"

"Why?"

"That is the question."

"Because I'm tired."

"You're tired?"

"Yes, tired. I'm old and just tired of the game. I work long hours, and am tired of coming home to an empty house."

"So you can't get laid back home?"

This comment caused Sal to smile.

"That's not it. At my age getting laid isn't what it's about."

"And what is?"

"Not being alone. Having companionship. Having someone to share things with, share life. That's it, that's all I really want. I lost my wife years ago, and since then I've realized that American women have changed. Or maybe i've changed and I just don't want to play the game. To me, this is straight up. It's business, and it can work out for the both of us."

"So, your answer is to buy a girl?"

"Sounds sad to you, but yes. As I said, this way both parties know where they stand. They both know it's about the money, so it's out in the open. I'm comfortable with that. I mean really, aren't most things?"

"What?"

"About money?"

Gavin thought about this. He didn't respond.

The guy was probably right.

"You don't care what people think?"

Again Sal smiled.

"When you're as rich as I am, you don't care about social decorum. Plus, there's not one man out there that won't envy me for a having a beautiful girl, a girl like one of yours on my arm. Plus, it wouldn't matter if I didn't pay for her or not, everyone would still think she's with me for my money anyway. Wouldn't you?"

Gavin smiled.

He was right.

"I'll give you that."

"And it almost seems that every girl out there is a gold digger. That they all care about money. American girls want too much!"

"You're right."

"So this is the route I chose."

"Okay, I can understand that. So is there a certain girl you would like to talk too?"

A question he would soon regret.

"There's one girl who has been sitting by your side the entire time."

Gavin began to get red.

He felt very uncomfortable.

"...I believe her name is Katka."

He couldn't be serious?

Gavin was about to say something, but before he did, Sal silenced him with one simple statement.

"I would pay any price for her."

"Keep talking."

"How much?"

Without hesitation, Gavin looked him dead in the eye and said, "Forty thousand."

Period. No haggling.

"Damn! You don't even flinch when you say that."

"There's nothing to flinch about."

"Most girls go for a lot cheaper."

"Most girls aren't Katka."

"She's that good?"

"Have you seen better?"

Sal shrugged.

"She's the best. Period."

"Okay, I'll trust you. But still, forty is pretty high."

"So then don't do it. Have a great day Sir, nice to meet you," Gavin said starting to walk off.

Gavin was pretty relieved.

He couldn't believe he had even taken it this far.

"Wait!"

The words he really didn't want to hear.

Gavin turned.

"I don't have time for this. There are others who are willing to pay that much."

"Is that right?"

"You're wasting my time. Goodbye."

"No, come on. Please have a seat."

Gavin looked and stared hard at him.

"Please," Sal said continuing.

Gavin sat down.

"Now, my first question to you is, can you get this high of a quality of girl all the time?"

"Why does that matter? We're talking about the here and now."

"I know that, but please, can you?"

"Of course. You saw the others."

"Because if you can, I can make you a very rich man. A very rich man."

Gavin wasn't prepared for this.

"Continue..."

"I have a lot of wealthy friends in my circle, and many of them have thought about his, but were kinda waiting to see how I fared. I can hook you up with them."

Gavin nodded his head, as he thought about this.

He was slowly being sucked in.

"But what about the now?" he then asked.

"Just tell me how you want to do this."

"Simple. You give me cash, Katka goes home with you."

"Just like that?"

"Just like that. It doesn't have to be complicated."

"I like that. No bullshit."

"No bullshit."

"When?"

"Whenever is good for you."

"I would like to spend a few more hours with her first."

"I can do that."

"And then we can take if from there."

"I'll need cash."

"Understood."

"When would you like to spend time with Katka?"

"How about tonight? Dinner?"

"Just dinner?"

"I already told you, sex isn't important."

Gavin smiled.

"God, I hope I never get old."

They both laughed.

"But listen Sal, seriously there are no test drives."

"Of course not."

"Then dinner it is. What time?"

"I eat early. So if we could do six, that would be great."

"Of course. So then, that's it for now?"

"I guess so."

"I'll have Katka come over at six."

"Thank you."

"No, thank you."

"And Gavin, remember, I can make you a very rich man."

That's a strange parting word Gavin thought to himself getting up to go.

But he also couldn't help but allow his imagination to run with this thought.

As he did he saw the jackass from the night before staring over at him and smiling.

Gavin ignored him.

Forty thousand dollars he thought to himself.

Forty thousand dollars.

So much had happened to bring them here with Dale and a day that seemed destined not to end well.

It all had happened so fast.

And here Gavin and Simona were once again caught up with one another. This time Gavin pushed her away.

Something he should have done a long time ago.

"Stop it! Get off!"

Simona looked confused, angry.

"We should get out of here. He doesn't seem that interested."

"Oh come on Gavin! You didn't see how excited he was when he was touching Miche!"

"I don't care. I can't go on with this. Too much has changed!"

"What? Meeka dying? It was her choice."

"It was her choice to die?! Yeah, i'm sure it was!"

"No, to go. Just like Katka did!"

Gavin again is injured by the words, the name. He closed his eyes in anger. When he opened them Dale was coming back into the room.

"So what's it going to be fat-fuck?!"

"For seventy thousand, i'm going to have to pass!"

Simona's jaw dropped when she heard the figure of seventy thousand. Her mouth voiced seventy to Gavin. He didn't look at her, but could feel her eyes burning through him.

He had constantly been raising the prices but this was just too extreme.

She could tell that the customers were getting seriously pissed.

"Though, I will pay you a few hundred to bang her. Maybe even go a thousand."

"What!? A few hundred to bang her?!"

"Yeah, I mean how about five hundred for a few rounds? Or a clean hundy for a blowjob?"

"What the fuck are you talking about? I'm not a fucking pimp!"

Dale smiled, even laughed.

"Well, kind of, aren't you?"

This angered Gavin to all hell.

"I'm a fucking business man!"

"Is that what you call yourself?"

Gavin was astonished, what was happening here?

Who the fuck was this guy?

"I don't know who you think you are, but you've crossed the fucking line. You better get the fuck out of my face!"

Dale didn't move.

"Listen, I was just hoping for something like what Sal brought back. Something like Katka."

Gavin walked right up to Dale, stared him down to the soul.

"There's only one Katka, and you my friend, will never have something like her."

Dale laughed.

"Will you again?"

"What?!"

It had been at least two weeks after Katka and Gavin had met. They were walking across the Charles Bridge, arm in arm, both smiling that smile that two people in love smile.

"I feel so comfortable with you."

"That's good, because we haven't been apart since that first night."

"Is that bad?" she asked.

"No, it's perfect. Yet, today I have to go to work."

"I'll miss you, can I say that?"

Gavin smiled.

That was so cute he thought.

"Yes you can, because i'll miss you too. I'll be thinking about you."

She smiled.

"Think dirty!"

His smile got bigger.

"I always do."

They kissed and held one another.

"And not so dirty too," she added looking at him with such endearment and affection that Gavin wanted to cry.

"You're absolutely beautiful," Gavin said just mesmerized by her beauty.

She didn't say anything.

"Okay baby, I gotta go. Pat's going to kill me if I no show again!"

"What if I asked you to stay?"

"I'd do anything for you."

This caused Katka to bite her lower lip.

She wanted so badly for this to be true.

She wanted so badly to have the fairy tale.

"Pick up another bottle of red on your way home?"

Red wine, he would never be able to drink it again without thinking of her.

Nor would he want to.

"Of course!" he said with a huge smile, "Okay I gotta run!"

"I know," she said turning sad.

They kissed one another one last time.

"But i'm not going to say goodbye."

She smiled to this.

"Never say goodbye."

"I like that," she responded repeating, "Never say goodbye."

With this she gave him one last big hug and kiss. He then turned to walk away, leaving Katka standing there.

"Gavin!"

Gavin turned quickly.

"I would do anything for you too!"

He smiled, she smiled.

"Then you go get a bottle of red too!"

They both laughed.

And he was off.

Later that night Gavin and Katka were back at Gavin's apartment. They were drinking and playing Monopoly. There were several empty bottles strewn around the place. Gavin appeared to have most of the money, and properties.

"Things are looking pretty bleak for you babydoll. Hotel on Park Place, looks like you owe me $1800, and I want all of it!"

"This game is so American! It's all about greed! Look at you! I don't have that much. And I don't have anything else to take off," she said with a big smile and flash of the goods under the blanket. "How much will you pay me for sexual favors?"

Wow, he thought to himself.

It was so hot the way she said it.

"What did you have in mind?"

With this she smiled, threw off the blanket and crawled over on all fours over to him.

"Whatever you desire."

"I desire you."

She smiled, licked her lips and then slowly maneauvered herself between his legs. Before she began she looked up at him and said, "This will cost you three thousand."

Gavin didn't answer, just smiled and puts his head back. He was in absolute ecstasy.

Soon visions of them together danced in his head and appeared on the walls of the apartment, like a black and white movie.

It was hot, too hot, to the point where he soon pushed her head aside and pinned her to the ground.

"That will cost you even more!"

"I'll pay anthing."

"Everything?"

He smiled.

"Everything."

"Promise?"

"Promise."

Katka smiled, almost looked like she was about to cry. She bit her lower lip, grabbed Gavin by the back of the head carefully.

"Gavin, I think i'm falling in love with you."

He smiled and brushed her face with the back of his hand.

"Are you still falling?"

Then they kissed and went at it on top of the Monopoly board. Money and properties flew everywhere or stuck to them as they rolled around on the floor.

After they were finished and lying there breathing hard Gavin said, "God, I wish I had this much money."

"Like you don't now."

Gavin laughed.

"I wish."

Not the answer she wanted to hear.

"But you do have some, don't you baby?"

The tone in her voice had changed to a more serious one.

Gavin picked up on this.

"Are you hung up on money?"

"Me?" Katka asked. "No not really."

"It seems so."

"Well I would say that I don't want to continue living poor. My family is very poor and," she said pausing, "Never mind. You're okay though right?"

"…no, not really. I had a rough past year."

"Oh."

"That's part of why i'm over here."

"Huh?"

"Yeah, I just wanted to get away from everything and come somewhere that's cheap to stay, and i'm really glad I did," he said pulling Katka closer to him.

"Baby, what happened back in the States? You still haven't told me."

There was silence.

"I still don't want to talk about it."

"Why not?"

"Because it still just stings. I'll tell you soon. But tonight I just want to enjoy this moment. I would take love over money any day."

"What if you could have both?"

"I don't think it's possible."

"Really?"

"Really."

"Why's that?"

"Money just causes more problems."

Katka didn't say anything, but she couldn't help but let her mind wander.

Sometimes where it shouldn't.

"Katka I need to talk to you," Gavin said having returned from the lobby where he had just met Sal.

It was the way he said it, Katka was immediately concerned.

"What's up baby?"

"Just come over here," he said taking her to another couch away from Simona and the other girls.

Simona looked concerned.

Actually, more angry.

"What's going on baby?"

They sat down.

"Listen, what do you think about all of this?"

She shrugged.

"I don't really. It's just another reality of living here. I've known lots of girls who have done this."

"So what do you think about us getting involved?"

"I think we could make some quick money, and good money."

"What if I told you that I just met a man who said that we could make even more money?"

"I would say let's talk to him. Simona has friends who want to go."

Gavin stared hard at her, uncertain whether he should say what he was about to say.

But he couldn't help it.

"What if that girl was you?"

The words just sat in the air.

The look on her face was one in which she couldn't believe what she was hearing.

"…excuse me?"

"Yeah, this guy downstairs, he's interested in you."

"And you said okay?"

"I didn't say anything."

Katka put her head down. She didn't know what to say.

Gavin started to doubt whether he did as well.

She looked crushed.

"Baby…" he started to say, but stopped.

Katka had begun crying.

"Gavin, let's just walk away."

There was silence.

"But baby, I think that…" the words trailed off, as she couldn't hear anything but her own tears.

She had no idea what else he said.

She would do anything for him.

Wouldn't he for her?

Wouldn't he?

Gavin stared at Dale in such a way that suggested Dale was in a lot of trouble.

Dale seemed to want to get under Gavin's nerves for whatever reason. Most likely because Gavin had been a major prick to him pretty much the entire day. That and the guys at home had become very annoyed with Gavin as of late, and thought that he needed to be shaken up a bit, brought back down to reality.

If possible.

"God, was she a good lay."

"What did you say?"

"What?"

"What did you say about Katka?"

Dale knew things were bad, and that there was no turning back. He proceeded down a road he would soon regret.

"Just what everyone says that's been between her legs!"

Gavin was floored and it took everything inside of him not to kill Dale with his hands at that very moment.

"Say that again!"

"Gavin...dont!" Simona screamed, scared, very scared.

They all looked at one another as if they all knew that a line had been crossed and there was no going back. The tension was high. Icy.

Nothing good would happen.

Doom loomed in the air.

Gavin turned back towards Dale.

"Say it again. I dare you."

Dale looked down and again knowing that he had no way out, and wanting to have some kind of dignity, he spoke up.

"What? That Katka can't get enough dick!"

Wham! Gavin striked Dale across the face, sending him flying to the floor, where he was quickly jumped upon by Gavin and seized by his fists. They came fast, hard, violent, with ill intentions.

"GAVIN NO!" Simona screamed.

She tried to stop him but couldn't.

No one could.

This was anger that had been brewing for months. Hatred from the deepest levels.

Pain only made better by more pain, and even then.

Finally Gavin stopped, only to ask a question in which he wasn't sure if he was prepared to hear the answer.

He was out of breath.

"….I thought Katka was married to Sal?"

Dale laughed and in doing so blood spit up out of his mouth and all over his shirt.

He sat there and smiled at Gavin in such a creepy, creepy way.

"She was until you got too greedy!"

Then Dale started to laugh uncotrollably. It was the look on Gavin's face that did it.

Lost. Blank. Unknowing, searching for answers, replaying the past in his head.

Nothing.

"What?!"

"You just kept pushing up the price, to the point where we decided that we needed to recoup some of our costs! Some girls relented, some ran, but Katka, she knew she had helped get many of the girls over, so she took it upon herself to pay off some of their debts."

Dale then paused, stared Gavin down, and then added, "I guess if you can fuck and get paid for it, why not right?!"

His smile reached from ear to ear.

"Especially if you love dick so much!"

Gavin began punching and kicking him again.

It was relentless.

Non-stop abuse.

Crushing blows and kicks.

Then he collapsed into the wall as visions of Katka raced through his head.

She had trusted him and had gone along with the plan.

What had happened?

What had he done?

That night at the strip club, when Gavin was taking a piss, some guy came up and started talking to him.

"Hello there."

"Hey," Gavin responded, hating it when guys wanted to talk to him while he was taking a piss.

Something about two guys holding their cocks while chatting it up, didn't sit right with Gavin.

He was always waiting to hear, "Hey, nice cock you got there."

"Hey you too, I see you shave…"

It was all too ridiculous.

Yet, the guy insisted on talking.

"You are quite popular here."

"I do their hair."

The guy laughed.

"You seem to know many of the girls?"

"They're my sisters."

This time no laugh, just a smile.

"Seriously though, I would like to talk to you."

"About?"

"About some of these girls coming over to the States to dance, especially that one sitting right next to you."

The anger began to flow.

He was talking about Katka.

"She would make a killing at my club."

"Oh, so you have a strip club?"

"Yes, many, but they are private and the guys love Eastern European women."

"That's great."

"She would be perfect."

"She is perfect, and she doesn't dance," Gavin said zipping up and walking away.

"We should talk," the guy shouted as Gavin headed out.

"We just did."

"They all dance," the guy muttered as the door closed.

"We'll talk again," he added washing his hands.

"I promise you that."

"Jesus Gavin, what's gotten into you?" Simona asked.

She couldn't believe what she had just witnessed.

Gavin didn't answer, just shook as tears swelled in his eyes.

He couldn't believe he was here, or what had happened.

His fists were throbbing with pain.

"Miche you can go."

Quickly Miche grabbed her stuff and headed for the door. It was obvious that she was pretty relieved and couldn't wait to get out of there.

"Gavin, come on, we should get out of here as well."

"No, you should. But wait," he said getting up. He grabbed the leather satchel full of money and threw it to her.

"Take it Simona, this is all you ever wanted."

She was shocked.

"It's not everything," she responded with eyes pleading a case for the two of them.

Gavin laughed.

"You gotta be kidding me?"

She shook her head.

"Just go."

She turned to leave but before she did, she turned back to him.

They stared at one another for a long time.

"Gavin, she did love you. She did. Very much."

There was a very long pause.

"But love isn't everything, is it?"

Gavin was floored.

It's what he wanted to know from the day she left, and at the same time what he never wanted to know.

Because he knew he loved her so much.

And now he was so scared she would never love him, not for all the things he had done.

"And that night with those guys from New York," she began then pausing to make sure he was listening, "She was trying to help you."

Wow.

"What?"

"Yeah, she was raving about your talents all night to them."

They were traders at a very successful firm.

As Gavin had once been.

Gavin's heart sank.

Why didn't she say something to him?

How did she even know, he thought to himself.

"Everything she did, she did for you."

Then she left.

Gavin could only think of one thing now. He knew what he had to do.

He turned to Dale.

"Where is she?"

"Who?"

"Katka."

"Either on her knees or her back."

Wham! Another blow to the face.

Gavin tried desperately to hold back his tears as visons of Katka and some other guy clouded his head.

"Just tell me. Please."

"Why don't you call Marco and ask him?"

"Whose Marco?"

Dale laughed.

"You're really not that smart are you? Obviously not if you sold your very own girlfriend."

Gavin was completely confused.

"What about Sal?"

"Sal isn't anyone of importance. It's Marco you really need to talk to."

"Who the fuck is Marco?" Gavin asked again, angry, even more confounded.

"Oh Gavin, did it not work out as planned?"

Gavin didn't say anything, as he ran everything through his brain, trying to backtrack.

What the fuck was going on?

What the FUCK had happened?

"Actually, I would say that everything has worked out perfectly. Well almost. Sal was right about you."

"Huh?"

Dale smiled.

Gavin had no idea what was coming.

"He said you would deliver. He said that he saw it in your eyes."

"What?!"

Dale laughed.

"Come on Gavin. He said the first time he said he would pay you big money, your whole face changed, and again when he gave you the money. He said we could count on you."

Gavin had no reaction.

"And you delivered."

Gavin felt sick.

"You just got too greedy, and forced our hand."

"What the fuck are you talking about?"

Dale smiled.

"It's just business Gavin. Just business."

It was about two months that Katka and Gavin had been dating when they were sitting on top of the hill by the castle over looking Prague at night. It was beautiful and from this view, it looked as though an artist had lit up Prague perfectly to be viewed from this spot. It was almost fairy tale like.

"Ideally, I would want to be taken care of. Not have to want for anything. I've never experienced that. I had a friend who did. She married an American. A very successful business man. She lives like a princess. Can I be your princess?"

"You are my princess."

"Would you take me to America one day?"

"Some day."

"I hope so."

"But i'm in no hurry to get back there."

"Don't you miss home?"

Gavin was silent for awhile, seeming to contemplate this question and how to answer it.

"I miss a lot of things, but right now it's best for me to be away."

"Baby why won't you tell me what happened?"

She had asked this question several times in the past two months, and still hadn't gotten an answer.

It was frustrating.

"Mainly because it's just really hard for me to talk about. I got fucked over, and I have so much anger about it. But the worse part is how my parents look at me now. The disappointment in their eyes brings me to my knees, and however many times I try to tell them that it wasn't my fault, I can tell they don't believe me. It kills me. Everything I did in life was for them."

Katka didn't know what to say, she just clutched onto him tighter as if to convey through her grip that she was there for him.

"I'll tell you someday baby, I promise. I just need to do it on my own."

"I understand."

"Thank you."

"You don't have to thank me."

"But I do. You've been the best thing that's happened to me in a long time."

"And you me."

"I love you."

"I love you too."

"Please just trust me baby."

"Do you trust me?" Katka then asked.

"I think I do, but it's really hard for me given what happened at home. But i'm trying really hard."

This seemed to hurt Katka.

"Baby I would never do anything to hurt you."

"I know," he said pausing, "Even if I wanted you too?" he then asked with a smile.

They both laughed.

"Well, maybe that. And I wouldn't hurt you. Or maybe just a little."

They kissed, it was deep, sensual. It said more than words ever could.

"Katka, every day I spend with you, makes me feel more and more like it would be impossible not to have you in my life."

"Aw."

"It scares me a bit, as I don't want to get hurt and i've been through too much shit lately that it would wreck me."

"Baby, don't think the worst."

"I know, i'm sorry. I never was like this before."

She kissed his arm.

"I'm trying."

She smiled.

"Well why don't you try just kissing me again?"

Dale was laying on the floor trying to wipe the blood from his mouth. Gavin looked even more worn-out and troubled. He appeared to be searching for the words, or courage to ask Dale a question, as he started and stopped several times. Finally he was able to muster the words.

"Did," he said pausing, not wanting to really say the words, "Did you have anything to do with Meeka?"

"Who the fuck is Meeka?"

"The girl who was found in the East River last week."

"Was that one of your whores as well?"

"She wasn't a whore. She was a really sweet girl."

"Just like Katka?" Dale asked like a smartass.

Gavin quickly kicked him in the gut. It was a good shot, as Dale squirmed in pain trying to find his breath. It took him awhile.

"You know this really isn't good for business," he said wincing in pain.

His face was really starting to show the affects of Gavin's fists at the moment.

It wasn't pretty.

"So did you?" Gavin asked again referring to Meeka.

Dale laughed.

"You do have to send a message every now and then."

That was it, Gavin unleashed a flurry of kicks and insults. He wanted to kill the man.

The only thing that stopped him was that he ran out of energy and collapsed onto one of the chairs in the room.

He was physically and emotionally spent.

Dale tried to speak.

"I thought the customer was always right."

"Shut the fuck up would you! I'm done with this shit!"

"You know they say, never make business personal and never conduct business when you're upset. You've broken both of those rules."

"I told you, shut the fuck up!"

Gavin pulled himself up, downed another drink, gathered his things and started to head out.

"Have a nice stay in Prague. You should check out the bridge."

Then he left.

He walked down the hallway, to the elevator and out of the hotel. Once on the street, he hailed a cab, jumped in and then flipped open his phone and dialed Pat.

"Gavin, what's up?"

"I'm going to go right a wrong."

"What are you talking about?"

"I think you know."

"Just walk away man."

"It's not that easy. I love that girl."

"They why…?"

"Not now Pat. Please, not now."

"You sound pissed off man."

"I am."

"You remember what happened last time you were pissed like this?"

The whole New Yorker night.

"Of course, i've been living it."

Katka went to meet Sal for dinner. On her way there, she thought about her and Gavin's plan and figured it could work, and that actually this was better than her plan with Simona. Now the money would only be split between her and Gavin.

The plan was simple, she wouldn't get on the plane from Amsterdam to New York at their layover. She would lose Sal in the Airport.

It was such a huge airport that it wouldn't be a problem at all.

Simona was not very happy with this at all, especially since Gavin pretty much out priced everyone and scared away potential buyers.

Oh well, Katka thought.

This was a one time thing.

Sal had made reservations at a very lavish restaurant for their dinner that night. The place was decorated with chandeliers lit by candles.

All the waiters were in tuxedos. Someone was playing a grand piano off in the corner.

Katka was very impressed and looked around to take it all in.

"Wow, this is a very nice place."

"This is my life."

"It's nice."

Sal smiled.

"Thank you for coming."

"No, thank you for inviting me."

"Believe me, the pleasure is mine. I haven't dined with a beautiful woman for a long time."

"And why's that?"

"My wife died ten years ago, and I've never gotten over it. My heart still belongs to her."

"That's very sweet."

"You remind me of her when she was younger. She was absolutely radiant, like you."

"Aw, thank you."

"Listen Katka, I wanted to have dinner with you to get to know you and for you to get to know me. The first thing I think you should know is that all I want is for someone who I can come home to and talk to. Honestly, I have a lot of money and will give you everything you desire and more. You'll never have to worry about not having enough money. Ever. Plus, I have a maid and a cook who does all the cooking."

"So what am I to do?"

"Whatever you desire. My only wish is that you're home when I get home and that you don't make me look like a fool."

"Look like a fool?"

"Yes, meaning to not sleep around."

"I am not a whore."

"I didn't say you were. But you are young and I know how it is to be young."

That same night Gavin and Pat were having a drink.

"I don't know what it is, sometimes I get this feeling like I can't trust her."

"Has she done anything that makes you think that?"

"Well besides that night with those jerkoffs, no, not really. But i'm still so angry about that night. It's just sometimes the way she looks at other guys."

"I've noticed that."

"Perfect. I was hoping that maybe I was blowing it out of perspective."

"Listen, she's just a friendly girl."

"How friendly?"

"Come on man, don't say that. That girl is totally in love with you. Yeah, she might look at other guys in a way that you're not too stoked about, but…"

"But what? That's the thing. I want her to look at only me like that."

"You've always been in love with the fairy tale."

"Is that so bad?"

"No, it just might not be realistic."

"I disagree."

"Listen man, can I be honest with you? I just think your confidence is shot right now and that you're over analyzing things. You've been through a lot."

"That could be."

"Because honestly, I've never seen you so happy with a girl. Actually, I've never seen you so happy, period."

"She does make me spin, I just wish I felt more confident about it."

"Maybe it's not her, and it's you. What more can she do? Speaking of, where is Katka now?"

"She's out," Gavin answered not wanting to tell Pat about what was going on.

Not now.

He knew what he would say, and he really just didn't want to deal with the drama at the moment.

"I think you two are great together," Pat said ordering another drink.

"Thanks man."

"You just need to think positive."

"Yeah I know."

❖ ❖ ❖

At the candlelight dinner Katka and Sal really seemed to hit it off. They were all smiles as they ate what appeared to be a seven course dinner, complete with the accompanying wine.

"So," Katka started, "You don't want to sleep with me?" she asked with a big smile.

Sal wiped his mouth with his napkin.

"I don't think I can. I'm sorry."

Katka smiled even brighter and touched her hand on his.

Sal was a really sweet guy.

She actually felt very comfortable and allowed her mind to wander into dangerous territory again.

And with what was going to come next, would only make it even more so.

"I can take care of you Katka, you and your family."

She liked the sound of that.

"I can also take care of Gavin. He'll become a very rich man."

Katka's ears perked up.

She really liked the sound of that.

"You really like him don't you?"

She didn't know how to answer this.

It just didn't seem appropriate.

"It's okay, it's obvious. I mean why shouldn't you like him? He's good looking, carries himself well, and just seems to have a je ne sais quo aura about him."

She smiled.

"He is a great guy."

Sal smiled.

"What's the most important thing to you?"

"What do you mean?"

"In life?"

Still Katka seemed confused. The question was pretty general.

"I mean like family, love, what?"

"Oh. I just want all the people I care about to be happy."

"Do you mean that?"

"Yes."

"And Gavin?"

"He's my world," she said unable to help herself.

Sal took a deep breath, paused, measured his words in his mind, and then dropped the bomb.

"You know about Gavin's legal problems don't you?"

What?

Katka sat up straight, eyes ablaze, "What are you talking about?"

Sal smiled a smile that said that he was about to talk about something rather embarassing, but that must be discussed.

"He hasn't told you?"

"No, he hasn't."

"Well I can see why he hasn't. The truth is that he really isn't to blame. He got pretty fucked in the entire deal."

This seemed to comfort Katka, and she thought about what he had said about his parents and how they looked at him.

"I don't know any of this."

"And it's not my place. But all I can say is, I can help him. I can make it all disappear. I can clear his name."

"How do you know all of this?"

"When you are a man in my position you make sure you know everything about who you are dealing with. I can get information."

"Oh my God," Katka said putting her face down and wanting to cry.

"Would you really do that for him?"

Sal chewed on his steak and nodded yes.

"And his parents would know everything? That he is cleared of any wrong doing?"

"Yes."

This was the greatest news she had ever heard. She was so excited for him.

"Why?"

"Because, I like you, and it's obvious you have a big heart."

A tear dropped from Katka's eye.

"I need that in my life."

Katka didn't know what to say.

"But we leave tomorrow."

What?

The entire game just changed.

When Katka got home that night, she found Gavin sitting out on the patio staring off into the night.

She looked at him differently now, the dinner had changed things.

She knew now what she had to do.

And it would be the hardest thing she had ever done.

Yet, truthfully, she hoped Gavin would tell her that they should walk away.

"How was it?" he asked as she walked through the door.

"He's a very nice gentleman."

"Yeah, seems to be."

She walked over and sat next to him.

She loved him even more now, having learned what she learned.

There was silence.

"So what do you think?" he asked.

"I'm sure it would work. What do you think?"

He didn't know.

"I think that I really love you."

"I love you too," she said grabbing onto him.

A tear formed in her eye.

"Promise?"

"Promise."

"Do you really want to go through with this?" he asked her in a way that suggested that perhaps they shouldn't.

This was the hardest question she had ever been asked.

"I think it will work."

"It's up to you. If for any reason you want to walk tomorrow, just give me a sign or say so."

"You too."

They were quiet for awhile.

"Baby," she began to say, "Everything will work out."

He forced a smile.

"I hope so."

"We just have to trust one another."

Then they kissed, and embraced.

They were one that night.

Inseparable body and soul.

The very next day Gavin and Katka went to meet Sal at his hotel. Sal was holding a leather satchel. He also had his bags packed. They all sat in the living room of of his suite.

"Well, I believe we can make this rather quick," Sal said sipping his coffee and looking at his watch.

"I agree."

"In this satchel is forty thousand American dollars."

"Perfect."

"And remember Gavin what I told you. I can make you a very rich man. As I said, I have a lot of friends and friends of friends who will be very interested in your services."

"I appreciate that. Referrals are always the best business."

"Basically it comes down to supply and demand. I can give you the demand."

"I don't deal with any shady characters though."

"Shady characters don't sit on Executive Boards, or host dinners for the President."

"You sure about that?"

They both laughed.

"Well at least these types have a lot of money, and forty thousand is a drop in the bucket for someone like Katka."

"Really? Well then, you are welcome to pay more!"

Sal smiled.

"So why me Sal?"

"Mainly because you're American, and there's also something about you that tells me that you like the finer things in life and like money. You wouldn't pass up good money for anything. Would you?"

Gavin didn't say anything. Katka stared at him, feeling torn between wanting to help him and wanting him to tell the guy to fuck off.

Yes, he was a nice guy, but now it just seemed like not such a good idea.

Sal continued.

"Exactly. See Americans understand the basic concept of greed. Like I said, it's obvious you like money and once you're exposed to it, there's no going back. In that satchel right now is forty thousand cash. The majority of Americans don't make that in a year. You've made that in less than two days with the promise of more to come. That's pretty amazing!"

"So how do you know I won't fuck you?"

Sal smiled again, but his smile was different.

He always covered his bets he thought to himself.

"Did you not hear what I just said?"

Then he laughed.

"Actually, go ahead an open the the satchel up."

Gavin did and was immediately awe struck at all the cash sitting in his hands. Katka looked very disappointed as she remembered him saying that money just caused more problems.

Gavin turned to look over at her, but only momentarily as his eyes averted back to the money.

He had never had so much at one time and thought to himself that this was enough to pay off his fines and perhaps settle things at home.

He could start over.

"That's what I thought. Granted I'm sure you've seen that much before, being in the business and all."

Gavin was speechless.

"I had a friend who had a fix on a game once. It was a sure thing. All of us loaded up on it except for my brother. He lost out on free money. Free money."

"But it's still a gamble."

"So is life."

"To an extent."

"Well, you're gambling now?"

"Yeah?"

"And it just paid off pretty big. You gotta seize your opportunities."

"Yeah, you're right."

"Well then. If that's it, then I think Katka and I need to head to the airport."

"So soon?"

"Yes. It was nice doing business with you. I will be in touch with you very shortly. I'll let you two say goodbye."

Sal got up and went to the other room, leaving Katka and Gavin by themselves. They stared at one another. They didn't say anything. They just stared.

Something was very different now, neither one of them knew what to say.

What to do?

It was all happening so fast.

Katka wanted Gavin so badly to say let's walk away, but he didn't.

He thought it was all up to her at the airport.

After all, wasn't it her that was risking the most?

And what did she really want in life?

Plus, Gavin was shocked they were leaving so soon, but even more shocked that he was holding so much money!

Sal came back into the room.

"I hope that was enough time?"

No answer.

"Alright then, Katka, let's go."

He extended his hand out to Gavin.

"Thank you Gavin. We'll be in touch. Goodbye."

They shook hands and then Sal headed to the door. He noticed Katka hadn't moved, hadn't taken her eyes off of Gavin.

"Katka honey."

Katka honey, Gavin thought.

This irritated him and he looked at Katka in such a way that she had never seen, nor liked.

She bit her lower lip, looked down for a quick second then looked up and said, "Goodbye Gavin."

It was direct.

Final.

Then she turned and walked away.

Gavin's jaw dropped, his heart stung.

She didn't really just say goodbye did she?

Gavin turned to look back at the money, only to look up just as Katka was heading out the door. She looked at him in a very awkward way. She looked utterly disappointed.

She walked out as Gavin muttered,

"Never say goodbye."

Gavin was in the taxi as it pulled up to the airport. He paid the fare, jumped out and ran into the terminal. He bought a ticket for New York and then headed to the bar. It happened to be the same bar Gavin sat at the day Katka and Sal flew away.

For as soon as she walked out and said goodbye that day, it hit him that he couldn't go through with it.

He just couldn't.

Could Katka?

He needed to know.

That day Gavin had arrived before them and had taken a seat in a bar near the security gate. He was careful not to be seen by Sal, though he was able to make eye contact with Katka, who had a very strange and alarming look on her face. They held eye contact for quite awhile.

As Sal and Katka made their way to security, they were still looking at one another.

He stood up and began to walk over.

He wanted to scoop her up in his arms and never let go.

But she shook her head, and looked down.

What?

Why did she do that he wondered?

She looked up.

She was a wreck.

"No Gavin," she mouthed, with tears in her eyes.

He was paralyzed.

As they walked through security, both of them closed their eyes, and were crushed. They both looked as if the wind had been knocked out of them. Sal seemed to be all smiles, and even caught a glimpse of Gavin, who he smiled over at and gave a little wave.

Gavin was destroyed.

What was happening?

More so, what happened?

A few moments later, that jerkoff that had peed next to him and again had approached him at the hotel passed by.

He too was all smiles.

What was he doing here Gavin thought to himself.

He began to panic.

The Rolling Stones, "I Can Almost Hear You Sigh" played on the radio.

He sat at the airport that day for hours, hoping that she would come walking back through the gate.

She never did.

Now he was back in the same bar, when his cell phone rang.

It was Sal.

"You fucking piece of shit! You lied to me! Where is she?"

"Hold on now, don't take that tone with me. I heard you had a bit of a temper tantrum."

"Where is she?"

"And you took the money as well, and gave it to that little money monger Simona!? Though I can't be for sure as Bill's voice was very gargled. Did you break his jaw?"

"He needs to lose some weight anyway."

"Well no worries about the money. It's yours anyway. I owe you that at least. The girls you've sold me cover that in a week!"

Gavin didn't know what to say.

"Why?" he finally asked.

"Business Gavin, it's just business. You should understand that. Let's remember that you're the one who sold your own girlfriend."

"It wasn't supposed to be that way."

"I know, but neither one of you did anything to stop it. I say we all got what we wanted. Or most of us."

"This isn't what I wanted."

"Are you sure about that? I haven't heard any complaints."

There was silence on the line.

"And remember, it has been over nine months. You've become a very rich man. You made this choice. You're the one who took the opportunity and ran with it."

The truth hurt.

"Will you tell me where Katka is?"

"Of course, it's the least I could do for you. Besides, your little friend Simona seems more than willing to pick up the reigns in your absence. Why don't you call me when you get back stateside. We'll do coffee, just like old time's sake. Have a great flight."

Thirty minutes later Gavin boarded his plane. Sitting in first class he thought back to the day everything went down, and how a week after he was sitting with Pat downing drinks at an amazing rate.

"You look like shit," Pat said.

"Thanks."

"No really. What's wrong?"

He told him everything.

"And you're still here?" Pat asked a bit worried and excited at the same time.

"It didn't go as planned."

"What do you mean?"

"I actually sold Katka. Katka actually got on the plane with the guy and went to the States."

"What?!"

"Yeah."

"I thought you said she was going to ditch him in Amsterdam?"

Gavin didn't answer.

"She didn't do it?"

"No."

"Wow!"

"Yeah."

"Oh my God!"

"I know."

"Why do you think she got on the plane?"

"That question has been ringing around my brain for the last five days."

"Wait, she was the one who set all this up right? It was her idea?"

"Not really, kinda, but not really. But what are you trying to say?"

Pat shrugged, wasn't sure whether or not he wanted to go down this road.

He had Gavin worried.

"You think she wanted that?"

"Maybe," Pat finally answered reluctantly.

"That's fucked! We were totally in love."

"Were you?"

With this Pat walked off. He couldn't believe what his friend had done.

Moments later Gavin's cell phone rang. It was a New York number.

Katka, he thought!

"Hello!" he answered excitedly.

"Gavin, how are you?"

It wasn't Katka, his heart dropped. The man continued.

"Actually I know the answer to that, Katka told me everything."

"She did?"

"Yes. I'm quite impressed, with the both of you. Mostly you though, and that's why i'm keeping my promise to call you, and make you a very rich man."

"Where is she?"

"Forget about her. Let's concentrate on the future. I have a friend who is coming over. Can you help him?"

"I don't think so."

"You mean you can sell your girlfriend but you can't sell a girl who wants to go? Or should I say can't be convinced it's a good thing to do." There was silence.

"I don't know."

"Katka said you should call Simona."

"Wait what?!"

"I'll call you soon with details. Goodbye now."

On the flight to New York, Gavin occupied himself having a few drinks, it seemed to be all he did now. There were a few girls checking him out.

He smiled.

Or tried his best to.

"Is your suit Prada?" one of them asked.

"Yes."

"Very nice."

"Thank you."

"What do you do?"

"Is it important?"

He couldn't believe he asked that question, and just by saying it he felt like half a man.

He had always believed that it was easy to make money, it was what you did that counted.

"I guess not. You're obviously very successful."

"I'm good at what I do."

He was.

How sad was that?

"I bet you are."

He smiled again, nodded to them, then turned to look out the window, where he watched the last year of his life play out like a movie. Eventually he fell asleep only to wake up to the plane landing in New York.

Once off the plane and in the terminal heading to the taxis, he dialed Sal's number.

"Hello?" a voice answered on the other end.

"Who the fuck is this?"

"Gavin, how are you?"

"Who is this? Where's Sal?"

"Sal's not here. And Sal's not important now."

"Well who the fuck are you?"

"I'm Marco, you remember? We met awhile back at the Hotel Inter-Continental. I told you that I could really use a girl like Katka."

"What?! Do you have something to do with all of this?"

"I told you that I own a lot of the strip clubs."

"So? Where is she? And where's Sal?"

Just as he asked this there was a voice in the background. It was Sal.

"Is that Sal?" Gavin asked feverishly.

Marco didn't answer, or at least not to Gavin.

"No Dad, I got it."

"Dad?!" Gavin asked wondering if he heard that correctly.

"Yes, sometimes a father knows best, and I guess he did, as you've been our best supplier."

"What the fuck is going on?"

"Gavin, now hold on. Now you didn't really think all of these girls were coming back to be kept women did you?"

Gavin was dead silent.

There was laughter from the background. It was Sal. Marco laughed a little as well.

"I think you knew. You just didn't want to believe."

"Where's Katka?"

"I would say from experience, probably getting fucked right about now."

"Fuck you."

"That's not very nice."

"Go get fucked!"

"That too isn't very nice is it?"

"Please tell me where Katka is."

"Why not. Let's meet?"

"Where?"

"You have money now, how about Hermes?"

"When?"

"Why not now? I've been looking forward to this."

Forty-five minutes later Gavin found himself at a very posh New York eatery, the latest hip and trendy place for all New Yorkers to dine, or be seen at. Marco was all smiles when Gavin arrived. Gavin was so angry, so embarassed at the same time.

Marco spoke first.

"First off, I would like to say thank you."

"Fuck you."

"You've given me the best girls. You've made me a very rich man. My customers love your girls. Then again, I guess I've made you quite wealthy as well," he added taking notice of Gavin's suit, cuff links, and watch.

"Let's cut the shit man, where's Katka?"

"What price are you willing to pay?"

"I'm not paying anything."

Marco smiled.

"Gavin, everyone has a price."

The words stung as he knew what Marco was implying.

"I'll buy her back for what you paid for her."

This caused Marco to laugh.

"Well isn't that nice of you. Yet, she grossed me ten times that. We way underpaid for her. Really didn't cost us a thing. What did it cost you Gavin?"

A tattooed soul.

"Remember, Katka is one of my most popular girls. The guys really love her, and from what I've heard, she seems to really love them!"

The tears began to form in Gavin's eyes.

"What's wrong Gavin? You realize you're in love with a whore?"

"Please, just tell me where she is."

"Listen, i'll make you a deal. I'll tell you where she is and let you talk to her. Then if you still want to do business, we'll talk."

"What do you mean if?"

"You heard me, if."

Marco then told Gavin where he could find her.

He really seemed to be enjoying this.

By the time Gavin showed up to the very private and secluded club that night it was packed. The place was filled with Wallstreet types, a lot of suits, and champagne was pouring throughout.

He waited and waited.

It was like being on death row.

Then all of a sudden the crowd went into a frenzy as Katka was introduced to the stage.

A guy turned to Gavin and said, "This girl is the reason i come, and cum if you know what I mean?"

Gavin wanted to strangle him.

And then there she was.

The stage was littered with money. Nothing less than a twenty. One man, an Asian man, just kept throwing hundreds. As each beat drummed on, Gavin felt his soul wither away.

It was the hardest three minutes of Gavin's life to watch.

At the end of the set, she disappeared behind a curtain at which point, Gavin was tapped on the shoulder and told to come to the back. He was led to a very lavish room with a very large overstuffed couch made of velvet.

He took a seat. Five minutes later Katka walked through the door.

She was carrying sex toys and condoms.

Gavin broke down and cried, he couldn't even look up at her.

"Oh baby what's wrong?" she asked not really looking at him, as she was setting down the items.

He looked up only to finally make eye contact.

Her eyes fill with excitement, panic, then sadness.

She collapsed into his arms, as if she was holding on to her very last breath for this very moment.

He held her tight.

He couldn't hold her tight enough.

They were both crushed and didn't talk for the longest time.

"Why did you get on that plane to New York?" he finally asked.

"I did it for you baby."

He was confused.

"What do you mean?"

Tears started cascading down her face.

"Baby what do you mean you did it for me?"

"Sal promised me he would help you."

And then it hit him.

Months after Katka left, he received a phone call informing him that everything would go away.

"What?" he had asked completely blown away at what he was being told.

The voice only answered, "Gavin, you have some very powerful friends. Keep up the good work. Good luck and goodbye."

That was it.

The call completely threw him off and he had no idea what had happened.

Well he did, but he didn't want to believe it.

And really he didn't care, because a few days later his parents called and were so happy and relieved.

"We're so proud of you," his mom kept saying over and over.

It was all too much.

He felt like the wind was knocked out of him.

Like life was draining out of him.

"Oh my God," he said to himself. "Oh my God," he said over and and over.

What had he done?

He felt sick.

"Baby, i'm going to be sick," he said then throwing up uncontrollably.

"You okay?" she asked rubbing his back.

He wasn't, and didn't think he ever would be.

There was silence.

"I think about you every day," Katka said clawing at him as if she couldn't believe it was him.

"I think about you."

"I just wanted you to be happy."

He cried and cried.

"Why didn't you tell me?"

"Cause you never told me Gavin and," she said trailing off as though she lost the words.

Gavin understood.

"Did you know that Marco was Sal's son?"

"Not till months later. That's why it worked so well, because he told me that he had several friends who would take care of my friends. So I told several of the girls back in Prague how much I was being taken care of and that they could trust you, all of them always liked you. They dreamed of having a guy like you over here, so the girls trusted Simona, just as long as you were involved. You were the perfect face man, for all involved."

"Why didn't you say something?"

"Because you never told me about your past, and that combined with the way you looked at the money..." she answered stopping to pause, as the moment got to her.

Anger actually began to creep in combined with the fact that she couldn't believe he was right here in front of her eyes.

Finally.

"And then when you didn't say anything on the phone that night, I figured everything worked out for the best...for most people."

Gavin didn't know what to say.

He was completely crushed.

The last few words destroyed him.

For most people.

"Then when you kept doing business..." she said unable to finish what she was going to say. She didn't need to finish. He couldn't bear to hear her finish.

He got the point.

And the truth hurt way too much.

Katka started to cry uncontrollably.

He just wanted to die in that moment.

"Why didn't you say anything that night on the phone Gavin? You just sat there on the line!"

"What was I supposed to say?"

"Anything Gavin. Anything. I needed something."

"And you? You could have said something?"

"Yes, but since that night with the guys from New York, you were different to me and I really needed to hear something from you."

"How do you think I felt? You made me feel as though this is something you wanted."

"Gavin all i've ever wanted to do was make you happy."

"I, I, you, should have…"

He didn't finish. He didn't know what to say.

There was nothing he could say.

"How did you end up here?"

She just looked at him, as if he shouldn't say anything further.

He would not be able to survive the answer.

"Oh my God," he said going white.

His tears came storming down.

"God i've missed you Katka."

She frowned.

"Why are you frowning?"

"You can't say that."

"Why am I here then?"

She was crying.

"Because I called you."

"That's not it."

She wanted to believe that, but it was so hard too.

It had been so long.

"Gavin, do you have any idea how long it's been?"

Gavin didn't answer.

"Almost ten months."

What could he say to this?

"You said goodbye to me."

"I know, because I thought it was."

There was a long pause and they just sat there staring at one another.

"So what now?" Gavin asked.

"I don't know. I think that's up to you. They made me work here to buy off my deal and Meeka's. All i've ever wanted was for you to be happy? Are you happy?"

He didn't have to answer this, the answer was written all over his face.

Five minutes later Gavin was outside the club with Marco.

Marco was all smiles.

"So Gavin, what's the word?"

Gavin just stared at him.

"How much?"

"What do you have?"

"What do you want? I'll give you everything."

Marco smiled.

"It's much more complicated than that."

The End.

Made in the USA